Time Traveller

Atlanta
Meets the
Cotton Slaves

Dan Whitehead

Seven Arches
Publishing

Published in 2012
By Seven Arches Publishing
27, Church Street, Nassington, Peterborough PE8 61QG
www.sevenarchespublishing.co.uk

A catalogue record for this book is available from the British Library.

Cover design, scans and typesetting by Alan McGlynn.

Printed in Great Britain

ISBN 978-0-9567572-2-7

'For Dillon and Daisy, my lines in history.'

Acknowledgement

A Huge Thank You To Ben Dempsey

Ben was one of the winners in our 2010 writing competition. When he was just eight years old, he bought the first book in our Time Traveller series and picked up a competition entry form at Waterstones in Wilmslow. His written entry was over 300 words long suggesting Styal Mill in Cheshire as a setting for a future book in our time travel adventure series.

He inspired the author, Dan Whitehead to write this book with his descriptions, such as the one below, of how children lived in the early nineteenth century when they were apprenticed to Mr. Greg the mill owner.

'The mill was really very noisy. It was so noisy that the children were deafened every single day. It was also very damp and pongy. It was so pongy that people actually wore washing pegs on their noses. The power was so powerful that people's fingers got chopped off and the machines still worked with lots of fingers stuck in them.'

Ben Dempsey, aged 8.

‹IF THIS IS THE FIRST TIME YOU HAVE READ ONE OF THE BOOKS THAT RECORDS THE ADVENTURES OF CHILDREN FROM THE TWENTY FIRST CENTURY IN A TIMEZONE DIFFERENT TO TODAY. YOU NEED TO KNOW›

> That SHARP stands for The Scientific History and Art Reclamation Programme.

> That STRAP stands for the Scientific Testing and Recording of Aggression Programme.

> That time slip is something that you might suffer if you travel through time and space, in a similar way to how some people get jet lag when they fly long distances on a jet air liner.

> That if you travel through time and space you are a xrosmonaut.

CHAPTER 1

An Unexpected Text

'Just leave me ALONE!' Atlanta shrieked as she slammed the bedroom door shut in her sister's face.

She rested her forehead on the cool, painted wood and let out a sigh. Geneva's footsteps were already thundering down the stairs. Next came raised voices from the living room. Geneva was telling their mum in exaggerated detail what had happened, no doubt saying what a bad attitude Atlanta had. Soon there would be footsteps coming back up the stairs, the slow methodical footsteps that meant her mother was on her way up. Sure enough, here they came, and then a sharp knock on the door.

'Atlanta! Open this door!'

Like most twelve-year-olds, Atlanta Tully had already developed a detailed catalogue of her mum's voices, and she could tell from the weariness in this one that it wouldn't be a serious telling off, just another *I expect better from you speech*. A heartfelt apology with a sheepish smile and everything would be fine. Atlanta took a deep breath and opened the door. Her still youthful, glamorous mum stood there, hands on hips, trying hard to look angry.

'What's this about you calling Geneva a gormless twonk?' her mum paused and then came the anticipated: 'I expect better from you, Atlanta.'

Atlanta clenched her teeth and tried not to roll her eyes. Normally she and Geneva got along fine, but her nine-year-old sister couldn't resist spicing up the story whenever they fell out, playing up her own innocence while exaggerating Atlanta's supposed wrong-doing. Atlanta considered trying to argue her case, explaining to her mother that she hadn't said anything like that and it was Geneva who had started it by bursting into the room and pulling silly faces. All she had wanted was to be left alone; sometimes that seemed like a crime in their house. But she saw the exhausted look in her mum's eyes and thought better of it. The incident would blow over far quicker if she just swallowed her pride and said sorry.

'Sorry, Mum,' she said, the regret in her voice quite genuine. 'I didn't mean to lose my temper.'

Martine Tully's face softened. 'What is it, love? You've been skulking around the house with a face like thunder for weeks. Is it the holiday homework? Is it...' She paused, as if unsure whether or not ask the question. 'Is it a boy?'

'Mum!' Atlanta protested, horrified at the very idea. Although, she almost wished that it was a boy. At least that would be the sort of everyday problem you could discuss with people, or share through cheesy movies and pop songs. But how do you tell your mum that the reason you were in a bad mood was because you were not being asked to travel back in time any more? How could you explain that, on a fantastic journey back into the past, you'd escaped from armed soldiers in the seventeenth century and then lived through an air raid in World War Two? And that now it had been almost a year since the strange girl from the future who arranged your trips into history had been in touch – and that your mobile phone no longer had a special screen that floated in the air and received messages across time and space. So that you were starting to wonder if you were actually going mad – that you had imagined the whole thing?

There really didn't seem to be any way of explaining all of that without looking completely bonkers, so she just shrugged. She hated lying to her mum, but the truth in this case would only cause more trouble. 'I'm just bored with the school holidays already. It's so exciting at Chets, I don't enjoy holidays like I used to when I was at primary.'

Just over a year ago, Atlanta's brilliance with the violin had earned her a place at the prestigious Chetham's School of Music (known as Chets) in the centre of Manchester, a bus ride away from where she lived in Moss Side. It was true that she really enjoyed being there, much more than at her primary school, where she used to get bullied because she was different. Chets was a very posh, very well respected school where some of the greatest classical musicians had played and trained. People from her estate never got to go to places like that, and Atlanta felt very special and privileged to be there. What wasn't quite true, was the fact that it wasn't just not being at Chets that made life seem so boring. Atlanta's relationship with excitement had changed forever when she'd met Mela in the museum on Oxford Road. Mela was a girl, who appeared to be the same age as Atlanta, but who wouldn't be born for thousands of years. Knowing that time could be folded flat, and journeyed through in the blink of an eye, was sometimes an unbearably exciting thought.

Mela had told Atlanta that she came from a time after something called the Dark Chaos, when all the knowledge of the world's history had been erased. She was part of an organisation called SHARP, or the Scientific History and Art Reclamation Programme. Atlanta had been chosen to join a top secret team of young time travellers, or agents as they were called, who voyaged back into the past to help rebuild the future of the entire human race. It was a dizzying idea and it still filled Atlanta with, not only fear, but excitement and wonder as well. Then, after just two trips back in time, it had all stopped. Her mobile phone, altered by Mela to send and receive messages across the centuries, hadn't received anything for one year two months, one week, four days and eighteen hours. Not that Atlanta was counting.

Mela had praised Atlanta's performance in her first trips, but now Atlanta worried that something had gone wrong. Maybe someone more important than Mela had taken a look at her adventures and been dismayed at this silly, frizzy-haired girl and her nervous first steps as a time traveller. Maybe it had all been a mistake. It had been a thrilling whirlwind of anxiety and celebration, but now boring, normal life had crept back in like a smothering fog and she felt lost and uncertain.

Her mum couldn't possibly have known any of this but, in the way that only parents can, she seemed to understand the emotions that Atlanta was wrestling with if not the reasons. 'Look,' she began, 'I know Geneva can be a handful, and I know you've got a lot to think about at the moment, but it's a small house and we all need to get along, otherwise we'll end up bouncing off the walls.' She reached over and gave Atlanta's shoulder a gentle squeeze. 'Give it some time, everything will work out fine. OK, love?' she said, her voice suddenly dropping to a whisper. 'And as for things being boring, I think that might just change.'

'What do you mean?'

'Never mind for now,' said Martine, giving a slightly mysterious smile which she changed quickly to a sterner look. 'Just don't let me hear you using words like that again to Geneva or anyone.'

'No, Mum, I won't. And I'm sorry, really sorry.'

Martine gave her a quick hug and a warm, tea-scented kiss on the cheek. Then she made a show of tidying up a rogue spiral of light-brown afro hair that had escaped from Atlanta's ponytail, gave another quick smile and headed back downstairs, where it sounded like Atlanta's little brother, Lincoln, was pounding his action figures into the letterbox.

Atlanta watched her go and realised she was still smiling. A natural, comforting smile that filled her up like warm honey. She was still frustrated and confused about a lot of things, but her mum had reminded her that there was always something more important to think about.

As Atlanta let her thoughts tumble around in her head, like mismatched socks in a washing machine, she heard her mobile buzz from her bedside table. Months ago the sound would have sent her scrambling to answer it, eager for news from the future, but she could tell without looking that it wasn't the unmistakable buzzing pattern of a message from Mela. Just a normal text. Probably from Simon, her best friend. She walked around her bed and picked up the phone, still lost in thought. She let out a gasp. The message said:

IS THIS ATLANTA TULLY? IF YES THEN TEXT BACK. URGENT!!! Danny H.

CHAPTER 2

An Unexpected Letter

Atlanta stood frozen to the spot. The mysterious text message stared back at her. Her mind raced through all the boring possibilities. Was it someone from school? She didn't think so. She didn't know anybody called Danny H. Certainly nobody who would know her mobile number or need to reach her urgently.

She felt a tickle deep inside her stomach, a giddy flutter of excitement. It was just an ordinary text, but it just had to be something to do with Mela and SHARP. There was only one way to find out. With fingers that trembled in anticipation, she hit *reply* and keyed in a response.

Yes. This is Atlanta. Who are you?

She hesitated before pressing *send*. She was uncomfortably aware that other kids didn't use proper spelling or punctuation in their texts and emails but, try as she might, Atlanta couldn't bring herself to type things like 'who r u?' It didn't make her very cool, but she was used to that by now. Frizzy-haired, mixed race girls who played the violin didn't get to be cool. Not at her old school, anyway. She bit her lip and sent the message. Only a few seconds later, her phone buzzed again, shaking in her palm like an angry wasp. It was another text.

Can u talk?

Atlanta desperately wanted to say yes, but she could already hear her mum setting the table, and the smell of cooking wafted up from downstairs. It would only be a few minutes before she would be called to come down for tea.

Not right now. Who are you?

She hit send one more time, and sat down on the edge of her bed. She could feel her heartbeat pounding in her head and forced herself to breathe slowly, calm down and wait to see what happened. Part of her still suspected it might just be one of the boys from school messing about, but deep down she knew that wasn't true. The phone buzzed again.

OK. Call u later.

'Atlantaaaaa!'

The shout from downstairs startled her so much that the phone leapt from her hands and she fumbled and juggled to keep it from falling to the floor. She made her way down to the kitchen and gave her hands a squirt from the antibacterial wash next to the sink. Geneva and Lincoln were already sat at the table while Martine flapped around them, putting out plates of food, the ketchup bottle and plastic cups of ginger beer. Atlanta joined them at the table and looked at her plate: chilli patties with rice and peas. Was her mum thinking about her dad again?

Atlanta's father had been killed when she was a baby, murdered by criminals who mistook him for someone else. Although she didn't remember him, she had dim memories of being a very young child, and seeing photos of a smiling black man on the mantle-piece. In one photo he was holding a trumpet – her father had been a musician, just like Atlanta, and in another he was standing with his arms around Martine. She thought that was their wedding day, but she wasn't sure. She also had a very vivid memory of walking into the living room one summer morning and finding her mum sitting on the couch crying, listening to an old CD. The music was bouncy and brassy – it was called ska, she learned later – and the CD cover on the floor showed her dad with two other men, wearing strange hats. She could still remember the tune.

But then her mum had met Travis, her new husband. He was Geneva and Lincoln's father and another musician. He worked on cruise ships and was away for long periods of time. Travis was really nice – a happy, fun-loving man, tall and thin with a smile that seemed too large for his face. Atlanta got along well with him, but her own dad was a subject that just didn't get mentioned. Most of the time she didn't think about it, but sometimes, like this teatime, Atlanta would sense that her mum was missing him, and a hole inside her would open up and ache a little. She had never plucked up the courage to ask what her dad had been like.

'Eat up, eat up,' Martine urged the family. Atlanta tucked into the crunchy yellow pastry of her pattie, scooping up some of the spicy beef filling from inside with it. The chilli in the patties made her tongue tingle, but they also made her feel strangely content.

Her mum had once said how much her dad had liked Jamaican food.

'Good news!' Martine suddenly blurted out a little too eagerly, as she finally stopped flitting around and sat down at the table. Three faces all stared at her, surprised.

'I got a letter from Aunt Bernie today,' she continued. 'How would you all like a holiday in America?'

There was second of stunned silence, and then Lincoln practically exploded out of his chair in excitement, while Geneva babbled a seemingly endless stream of, 'oh my god' and, 'no really?' Neither of them stopped to ask who Aunt Bernie was, even though, outside of a regular Christmas card, they never heard from her. What mattered were the words 'holiday' and 'America'.

For Atlanta, it was a little more complicated. She knew Aunt Bernie was her dad's sister. She lived in a place in America called Atlanta, which was where her own name had come from. Her dad's side of the family were rarely spoken about, and she had the impression that her mum's family, particularly her nana in Prestwich, hadn't gotten along with them that well.

Even so, the news was exciting enough to push

all thoughts of cryptic text messages and time travel out of her head for a few minutes. Going to America was one thing, but the chance to meet her family – her dad's side of the family – was even more exciting. And, she realised, it was a little terrifying too. She turned the information over in her head. Martine was trying to keep Lincoln in his chair while he bounced around like a puppy, sloshing ginger beer over his pattie, and at the same time she had to argue with Geneva that, no, she couldn't go and tell her friends until she'd finished her tea.

Once things calmed down a little, and she was sure that the excitement wouldn't erupt again, Martine told the kids more about their trip. 'Aunt Bernie wrote to me a few weeks ago,' she explained. 'Her father-in-law died earlier this year and left her some money. She really wants to see us, and she said she'd pay for us to fly over and stay at her house. There are still a few weeks until the summer holidays are over, so I thought it would be a nice break before you all start back at school.'

'When are we going?' asked Atlanta.

'The week after next. Aunt Bernie has ordered the tickets and they should be here in a few days. Oh…passports! Oh God, where did I put them?'

Tea was finished quickly, what with the holiday news hanging over the table, and they were just finishing their yoghurts when Atlanta's mobile buzzed against her leg. She'd been in such a daze from the mysterious text messages that she'd shoved the phone into her jeans without even thinking about it. Mum had a strict rule: no phones at the table. Geneva had clearly heard the noise, and she looked at Atlanta with an arched eyebrow, letting her sister know that she could get her in trouble at any time. Atlanta gave Geneva a pleading stare and pressed her hand to her pocket to try and muffle the buzzing. It wasn't stopping. This wasn't a text, it was a phone call.

Panicking now, Atlanta hurriedly spooned in the last mouthfuls of yoghurt and quickly got up. 'Er... going to the loo! Emergency!' she mumbled and dashed back upstairs before her mum could say anything.

In the bathroom, Atlanta slid the bolt across. Desperate for every last scrap of privacy, she climbed into the bath and pulled the blue, seashell curtain across. She knew it wouldn't make any difference if anyone came banging on the door, but it made her feel safer and more secretive. She fumbled in her pocket for the still-buzzing phone, almost dropping it in the bath in the process. There was a little puddle of water near the plughole that was soaking into the seat of her jeans, and she shuffled awkwardly from side to side to get away from it.

The screen said: UNKNOWN NUMBER. Atlanta hit the answer button and nervously held the phone to her ear.

'Hello?' she said, slowly and cautiously.

'Atlanta?' replied a boy's voice.

'Yeah, I'm Atlanta,' she said. 'What do you want?' The question came out snappier than she intended.

'Phew!' laughed the boy. 'I thought you'd never answer! I'm Danny. Danny Higgins. We need to talk. In real life, I mean, not with texts.'

'Oh... OK. Hi. Er... nice to meet you. I'm Atlanta. But, oh yeah, you know that. Sorry,' Atlanta said, the words tumbling out of her mouth far too quickly. The boy called Danny laughed again, a friendly chuckle that made her feel a little bit better, but also even sillier for her frantic gibbering.

'What I mean is, who are you?' she asked.

Now it was Danny's turn to apologise. 'I thought you knew!' Danny replied. 'I'm a time traveller too.' He said it in such a matter of fact way, like he was telling her his favourite ice cream flavour, or what he watched on TV last night. Atlanta tried to hide it, but couldn't help letting out a gasp of astonishment.

'Oh, right. Of course,' she said, trying to sound cool, as if she had conversations about time travel every day. Conversations about time travel with strange boys, while sitting in an empty bath. She couldn't help smiling. Life had certainly become a lot stranger since Mela and SHARP had entered her life.

'Oh, bum!' whispered Danny suddenly. 'Someone's coming. I've got to go. Meet me tomorrow. Lunchtime. The same place you first met Mela. I promise it'll all make sense then.'

'OK, but how will I know who you...' Atlanta began, but the line was already dead. She held the phone in her hand, drops of cold bath water still soaking a dark patch on her bottom, and forced herself to take a deep breath. The same place she had met Mela was the coin room in the Manchester Museum. After months of waiting, the adventure was starting again!

CHAPTER 3

Stabilising The Neutrino Flow

The museum was not far from her house. Inside, it was cool and quiet compared to the hot, itchy bustle outside. Atlanta made her way up the stairs to the coin display room. There was no one there, and she soon found herself lulled into a relaxed state by its serene atmosphere. Her footsteps echoed on the hard, wooden floor, and the sound of traffic from outside was muffled into a low, murmuring hum. Tiny flecks of dust danced in the sunlight streaming in from the window. Atlanta closed her eyes and took a deep breath, drinking in the peace and quiet. Not many people came to look at old coins and that was one of the reasons why she'd always liked being in the coin room, even before it became the starting point for her life as a time traveller.

Atlanta ran her fingers over the cool glass and old wood of the nearest display case, worn smooth by years of visitors; she peered in at the tiny bronze, silver and gold discs inside. Her favourite was an old Roman coin, less than a centimetre across. It was a dull, muddy brown colour. The image on the front was almost worn away, though it looked like a staff, or maybe a tree. It was a quadran from 41AD, which meant it was worth a quarter of a full coin.

She wasn't sure why she was drawn to this unassuming bit of old metal more than the others, but she liked how battered and used it looked. It seemed to have had a busy life. Almost two thousand years ago, that coin had been carried and passed around by people, who had long since turned to dust. It had been used for buying and trading and saving, by people completely unaware that their possessions would end up in a glass box in the year 2012, pored over by strangers. That thought amazed her, and she began rubbing the handful of coins in her own pocket. Where might they end up in another two thousand years?

She was startled from her daydream by a voice behind her.

'Think they've got enough for a Coke? I'm gasping.' Atlanta spun around and found herself face to face with a boy about the same age as herself. His sandy hair was sticking up, like he'd just got out of bed, and a cheeky grin spread warmly across his face. He stuck out his hand.

'Hi Atlanta. I'm Danny. Nice to meet you!'

'You made me jump!' she laughed. She shook his hand. 'And, er, nice to meet you as well.' Atlanta didn't usually meet boys, apart from Simon, her best friend, and she'd certainly never met a boy to talk about time travel, so she had no idea what to say next. There was an awkward silence.

'Pretty weird, eh?' said Danny.

'Huh?' replied Atlanta.

'All these old coins,' Danny replied. 'In fact, everything in this museum. It's almost a shame that they're all locked away behind glass. Makes them look stuffy and boring. You forget that these were just normal things for normal people. I wonder who was the last person to spend them, before they ended up buried, waiting to be dug up and put on display?'

'I was just thinking that! Do you think we'll get to meet them? The people who had these coins?' She paused. If there was a clumsier way to drop the subject of time travel into the conversation, she couldn't think of one. Danny laughed again, louder this time.

'I don't know!' he chuckled. 'That would be awesome though. I hated doing history at school, but now I think it's pretty amazing. I've read quite a bit about the Romans; they were pretty cool.' He stopped and smiled. 'So where have you been? Or, you know, *when* have you been?'

Atlanta started telling Danny all about her first time travel adventure, how she'd travelled back to 1631 and helped Sir Humphrey Chetham escape from the King's soldiers down a secret passage in a well. Then she told him about her second journey, to the night in 1940 when German planes had bombed Manchester Cathedral. She told him how scared she had felt, but also how exhilarated.

It felt good. No, better than that, it felt great to actually talk to someone about her amazing adventures, someone who wouldn't think she was crazy.

Danny told her about his first encounter with a guy from the future called Kaz, and his journey back to Bramall Hall in Tudor times, how he took part in a contest against a boy in 1588, and the problems he encountered in 671 AD, a period called the Dark Ages, when he had found himself stranded in an Anglo Saxon forest full of wolves!

'Wow!' gasped Atlanta, 'That sounds really scary. I think I got off lightly with soldiers and bombs.'

'I don't know, at least you can see a wolf coming and try to hide.'

'Yes, I suppose so. Did your contact, Kaz have that strange thing of more than five fingers?' Atlanta held her hand out and looked at it, as if convincing Danny and herself she only had five.

'Yeah, they have seven digits on each hand. On my first meeting with Kaz, he held his hand up to show me – it was what finally convinced me that he was from the future. I've got used to it now, but I thought it really weird at first.'

'Me too.'

'Well the thing is,' Danny continued, 'I've been sent by SHARP to talk to you about your next journey. The reason you've not heard anything from Mela is because they're having problems. There's another time travel outfit called STRAP, and it seems like they're deliberately mucking up SHARP's systems, hacking into stuff, taking over time streams. STRAP's already sent a boy called Alex back to a rebellion at Edinburgh Castle, in 1314 I think, and it sounds like they didn't care if he came back alive or not.'

'That's horrible!' said Atlanta. 'Was he OK?'

'He got back all right in the end, but it sounds like SHARP is really rattled. How much do you know about them?'

'Not much,' admitted Atlanta. 'Only what Mela has told me. They're trying to reclaim art and history from the past because of something horrible that happens in the future, wiping all the records.'

'Yeah, the Dark Chaos,' interrupted Danny. 'No idea what that is, or more importantly when in the future that happens, but it sounds pretty bad. Sometimes, I get pretty horrid thoughts that it might be just a few years away and that we will be living through it.'

'Oh! I'd not thought of it like that!'

'Sorry, I shouldn't have got on to that subject, but it is one of the reasons I do all this stuff. Anyway, my contact, you know Kaz, who I just told you about, was able to get through to me because my phone was the first one they altered. It had been exposed to the time stream longer and built up a stronger connection, so STRAP's interference had less of an effect. At least, that's what they told me.'

He rummaged in his pocket and brought out a chewing gum wrapper. On it was written a long series of numbers and symbols. 'They've given me a code that will make your phone work again by, er, re-routing, something called the quantum tunnel effect using a...Heisenberg bridge, I think, to stabilise the neutrino flow... I try to listen to what they tell me but to be honest I don't really understand any of it. I wish I did but the science is probably even beyond the guys who are studying this stuff at our universities.

Atlanta nodded as Danny took her phone and entered the code. The phone chirruped and burped in response. Danny cocked his eyebrow at the device.

'There,' he said. 'I think that was a good noise. Did that sound like a good noise to you? Give it a try.'

Atlanta activated her phone and the futuristic screen that Mela had installed expanded and hovered in her hand. Almost immediately, a message from Mela came through. Atlanta grinned and couldn't help but start to read it.

'Yep, that works,' laughed Danny, moving to shield Atlanta from the doorway in case anyone was passing and demanded to know how two kids had managed to get a holographic phone from the future. 'Probably best to put it away and find somewhere more private before doing that again,' he added.

Atlanta quickly switched the phone off and slipped it back into her pocket.

'Thanks, Danny,' she said. They began making their way out of the coin room, down the stairs and out into the museum lobby.

'Look, I've got to get going,' said Danny, almost apologetically, as they reached the large double doors at the museum entrance. 'But you've got my mobile number now, so let's keep in touch, yeah? I've got a blog too, so Google me and let me know how you get on with your next trip.'

'I'd like that,' said Atlanta and waved as Danny strolled off into the sunshine. He gave a quick, friendly wave in return, and then disappeared around the corner. Clutching her phone tightly, she hurried to the bus stop and waited for the bus home. It felt like hours before the number 86 chugged into view, but she knew it could only have been a few minutes. All the time, her fingers danced and jiggled the phone around in her pocket; impatient to open it up and see what messages from the future awaited her.

Atlanta hopped aboard the bus as it hissed to a stop, flashed her pass and quickly made her way to the upper deck. As she had hoped, the hot weather meant most people had decided to walk, and the seats were all empty. Usually Atlanta avoided the top deck on the bus where the rowdier kids sat, especially when going to school, but right now her need for news from Mela drowned out her natural desire to steer clear of trouble. She scrunched down behind the seats at the back, and flipped her phone open.

Hi Atlanta. If you are reading this it must mean that

Danny was able to make contact and apply the update to your phone. Apologies for not being in touch sooner — things have been a little crazy here. I wish I could explain more but it is very complicated. I hope you are well and still want to be a part of the SHARP programme. I will be waiting for your reply. Mela.

Atlanta was so pleased to get the message, she beamed a huge smile at the empty bus, and then went back and read the message again, more carefully this time. She realised her heart was beating like the timpani section of the orchestra. She forced herself to calm down before typing her reply.

Hi Mela. So glad to hear from you. I was worried you didn't need me any more. I'm ready for another mission as soon as you have one!

She looked up suddenly as two young boys climbed the steps onto the upper deck, but they sat near the front and carried on an intense conversation about who they thought had got into the game they had just been playing. Atlanta ducked back down and read her message again. Was it too eager? Not eager enough? Should she play it cool? She considered deleting it and starting again, but then told herself off for being silly and hit send before she could waste any more time worrying about it. Almost immediately, a new message arrived.

Thank goodness! I was so worried you would want to stop! There's a new mission waiting — I've been holding the time window on standby, saving it for you! Details will arrive shortly. Mela.

Atlanta flipped the phone closed and let out a gasp of relief. She was going to travel through time again! She beamed a contented smile, closed her eyes and rested her head on the hot window as the bus carried her home.

CHAPTER 4

A Window Into The Past

Atlanta was so excited as she made her way from the bus stop to her house that she had to stop herself from breaking into a run. There were practical matters to attend to. When she had first taken the job of time traveller for SHARP, Mela had made it clear she should always make sure that, when she made contact or took missions, she wouldn't be disturbed. There was little chance of that, though, in her small house; someone was nearly always around. After waiting so long, Atlanta wasn't sure she could wait to be safely alone, and she was worried that her opportunity might pass.

She allowed her hopes to rise, though, when she neared the house; it seemed quiet, and the downstairs windows were closed. Surely, on such a hot day, that must mean there was nobody home? Maybe her mum had taken Lincoln to the park?

Her hopes crumbled as soon as she put her key in the door and stepped inside. The sound of cartoons came from the living room and, sure enough, when she peeped her head around the door, there was Lincoln, sprawled across the carpet, surrounded by toy cars, action figures and the crumbs from a packet of smoky bacon crisps. Atlanta didn't want to get dragged into a Lincoln conversation so she tried to quietly withdraw, but he heard the floorboards creak and rolled over.

'Hey, 'Lanta!' he yelled. 'I can do an ultra mega karate chop. It can chop down robots! Want to see?' Atlanta couldn't help but smile back – Lincoln was the sort of energetic little brother who could squeeze wide-eyed excitement and fun out of thin air.

'Maybe later,' she said. 'Why don't you open the windows?' she added, still a little annoyed that this small detail had allowed her to get her hopes up.

'Wasps,' whispered Lincoln, conspiratorially. 'Space wasps!'

Atlanta nodded, as if the explanation made total sense, and headed for the kitchen where she could hear the *whump, whump, whump* of the washing machine. When she walked in, she found her mum sitting at the dining table, surrounded by neatly folded piles of clothes. A red plastic basket, rather cracked and worn, sat at her feet, still half-full of clothes waiting to be ironed. She hurriedly shoved something into her pocket at the sound of Atlanta's entrance and wiped her eyes on her sleeve. It looked like she'd been crying.

'Are...are you OK, Mum?' Atlanta asked, all thought of time travel disappearing in an instant.

'I'm fine, love,' replied her mum, sniffing. 'I was just being silly.' She took her hand from her pocket and Atlanta saw that she'd been looking at a small photograph. It was slightly crumpled from being shoved away in a rush, so her mum placed the photo on the table and gently smoothed it down. Atlanta walked over and looked at the photo.

It was a picture of her mum and dad. They were both smiling big, happy smiles that shone from their eyes. Her dad had his arm around her mum's shoulder, and she was resting her head on his chest. They were in a park somewhere – Atlanta didn't recognise it – but it was clearly a long time ago; her mum looked much younger.

Atlanta studied her dad's face. She could see something of herself in his features, in the curve of his nose and the line of his brow. She walked past the photo of him in the living room every day, but had almost stopped noticing it. This was a picture she'd never seen before, and it had a powerful effect on her, as if she were looking back into a window in time. That thought snapped her to attention. The crazy idea crossed her mind that she could go back in time and meet her dad. Could she go back and stop him from going out on the night he died? Could she save him?

Her mum's hand on her wrist pulled her from such manic thoughts.

'You alright, sweetheart?' she asked tenderly. Atlanta realised she had tears in her eyes. She blinked them away.

'Yeah, I'm fine Mum,' she replied. 'I just...' She struggled to put her feelings into words. 'It's just that sometimes I forget to think about Dad, and then I feel bad about it, but then I can't remember much about him.'

'You were so little when he died, and I know we don't talk about him very much. It hurts so much when I think about him that sometimes I forget that you miss him too.'

Right at that moment, Atlanta felt her phone begin to buzz. Mela was sending through her mission details and they'd only be active for a short time.

'This trip to America,' her mum continued, 'It's brought up a lot of old memories and feelings for me. It just got on top of me for a moment then, but maybe you're old enough now to understand.' Atlanta tried to ignore the buzzing in her pocket, but it felt like it was getting louder and more insistent with every second. She desperately wanted to stay with her mum, to have this conversation that had been many years overdue, but she really wanted to see Mela's message as well.

In the end, Martine's practical attitude gave her the way out. 'Look at us,' she sniffled with a sad smile, 'crying in the kitchen like we're on Coronation Street or something. Your dad wouldn't have stood for this. He'd put on a song and drag us out into the garden to dance until we cheered up.' Atlanta smiled at this thought. It felt like a little fragment of something important, a bitter-sweet glimpse of a life she'd missed out on.

Martine gave Atlanta a kiss on the cheek and a squeeze, and then busied herself with the washing basket. 'Anyway, I must get on. Lincoln's underpants won't wash themselves, more's the pity,' she laughed. Atlanta smiled too.

'I love you, Mum,' she whispered.

'You'll set me off again!' Martine gave her a little push in the direction of the door. 'Go on, get off to your room and do whatever it is you youngsters do with all your wonderful free time.' She put her hand to her forehead in a theatrical gesture, as if she was about to faint. 'Just leave me here, with all these underpants!' she gasped. 'I'll manage somehow...' She swooned into the kitchen chair, then shot Atlanta a wink. Atlanta gave a grin in return and bounded upstairs.

There was no sign of Geneva – she had probably gone to the shops with her friends – so she ducked into her bedroom and flipped open the phone. She pressed the black button that activated its special time travel features and the screen slid away from the phone, expanding to the size of a reading book. A message blinked on the screen.

‹Hello again, Atlanta. Welcome back to SHARP›

Although at the start of your work with us, we provided you with detailed information about SHARP, we feel we need to update you a little. Some points you may have forgotten and others might have changed in the intervening time.

Our policy has not changed. We still hold firm in the belief that it is possible to travel back safely through time to bring about the greater good for all humanity past and present.

‹Pre-Travel Information›

Please read all our instructions carefully. You will need to locate the time/space bag we will have left for you in the usual place. Your unique agent number is the same as for your previous trips: 15799.

‹Travel Information›

We cannot emphasise enough the importance of being alone and somewhere safe before setting out, and of no one missing you. We are still aiming at our young 21st century time travellers only being away from their own time for four to six minutes. This allows for several hours, or possibly days, in the time they have travelled back to. However, under difficult conditions the time away in your present might be longer. Because of this, try to make absolutely sure no one is likely to notice, or be worried, by your departure.

You know that it is more difficult, though not impossible, for us to transport bodies wearing clothes, so 'strip down to underpants or swimsuit for girls' is still the instruction.

Our material scientists have been working wonders with the travel bag and it is now lighter and more flexible than ever. When it is stuck to your side, you really will not feel it. Remember to do this before you leave. We have had trouble with a time traveller forgetting to put the camera disc on their forehead and so the whole journey was a waste of time, power and money because nothing was recorded! So remember, on arrival, however dreamy or dozy you feel (and we do know this is one of the effects), take the silver disc out of the time/space bag and press it to your forehead. When the backing disc comes away, leaving just the film on your forehead, do put this back in the bag. These are actually quite expensive and easily re-useable.

‹Return Journey›

We appreciate that there can be dangerous situations and the emergency procedure of keying in your dedicated number of 15799 and then pressing the red button sometimes has to be used, but do try to only come back when you feel the phone vibrating which means that your return has been activated by us in the most cost-effective way.

‹After Your Visit›

We will, of course, contact you after your trip to let you

know how you have done.

Here are the instructions for your current travel option

‹Time Zone›
August 1836.

‹Place›
Cheshire, England.

‹Landing›
Upper floor of Apprentice House.

‹Instructions›
Retrieve period clothing from beneath bed. Follow apprentices in their daily routine.

‹Destination›
Quarry Bank Mill, a textile factory owned and run by Robert Hyde Greg, a wealthy businessman.

‹Identity›
Lucy Garner, an 10-year-old apprentice at the mill.

‹Conditions›

Weather fine. Political and social situation stable.

<Equipment>
Mobile phone. Travel bag. Phone fitted with beam of
light for emergency use only. Activate by keying in
T-O-R-C-H.

If you are ready to travel, do as follows:
›Take off clothing, except for underwear or change into
swimwear.
›Press time/space travel bag to your body until it at-
taches.
›Key in 15799 and press the green button.

Good luck.

Atlanta placed the phone on the bed and reached
into the bottom of her wardrobe, where she kept an
old shoebox with 'sheet music' written on the lid en-
suring that Geneva and Lincoln would leave it well
alone. It was in this box that SHARP left the necessary
equipment for time travel and sure enough, there inside was the small pouch, the time/space travel bag.

Inside the time/space bag was a small silver disc,
a bit like a tiny CD. This was the sensor that allowed

her to transmit everything she experienced – every sight, sound, smell and taste to the people in the future. Atlanta changed into her old swimming costume, which she could wear under her clothes in the past without suspicion. Then she pressed the time/space travel bag to her stomach, where it stuck. This would remain in place during the trip and would allow her to keep her phone with her at all times, even once she'd changed into clothes from the period she was travelling to.

She thought about the mission information and realised that she was a little disappointed. Going to work in an old mill, making cloth? That didn't sound like much of a challenge. In fact it sounded really easy and pretty boring. But, Atlanta reasoned, it was still a trip back in time. It would be silly not to be excited. She grabbed her phone off the bed and slipped into the bathroom, where she locked the door. She knew that no matter how long she spent in the past, only a few minutes would pass in the present day. With Mum busy with the washing, Geneva out with her mates and Lincoln lost in his cartoons, she figured that, even without complete privacy, she should be safe.

She keyed in her code number, 15799, took a deep breath, closed her eyes and pressed the green button. She heard a faint, far-off, high-pitched whine coming nearer and nearer, filling her ears. Then... Nothing.

CHAPTER 5

The Apprentice House

A slight jolt. Then darkness. Atlanta had to rub her eyes to make sure they were open, so complete and ink-black seemed the darkness surrounding her. Next came the smell, a tangy, sweaty stink. And then the noises: dozens of quiet breathing sounds, punctuated by occasional snorts and moans.

Atlanta froze. Where was she? She strained her eyes against the blackness. As they adjusted, she realised there was a large window to her right, an arch of dark blue rectangles that stood out slightly from the blackness of the room. Slowly, she began to make sense of the shapes around her. She was standing in a very small space between what looked like rows and rows of boxes in a long, narrow room. The gaps in between the boxes were just wide enough for a person to shuffle through, if they turned sideways. Then she realised they weren't boxes at all, but crude beds with high, wooden sides. In each one, she could now detect the unmistakable lumps of people sleeping, two to each bed.

Uncomfortably aware that she was only wearing her swimming costume, she knelt down carefully and began feeling around on the hard, wooden floor under the nearest bed for the clothes she would have to wear. As her fingers explored, they brushed against something cold and hard. She gave it an exploratory flick with a fingernail and it clinked like a china bowl. A sloshing sound came from within, along with a sudden, sickening whiff that reminded her of a farm. Oh no! She realised it was one of those pots they used to wee in ages ago, and a full one at that. It took all of her willpower not to cry out in disgust.

Her fingers quickly danced away from the primitive toilet and landed on a bundle of cloth. She snatched the cloth from under the bed and discovered it was a simple dress. She could see more clearly now because the dark blue of the window was slowly growing lighter. She quickly threw the dress over her head. Then she took out the small disc inside the time/space bag that was attached to her stomach and pressed the disc to her forehead. The backing came away and the film merged into her skin, as she knew it would. She fumbled under the dress, put her mobile in the bag and snapped it safely shut. Then she squinted at her surroundings. There was one person in the bed behind her, leaving room for one more, the only available space in the whole crowded room. It felt weird to be climbing into this cramped little space next to a stranger, but Atlanta swung herself over the side of the bed, as quietly as she could, and lay down. The bed was hard and lumpy, with a scratchy blanket and a mattress filled with straw that poked and prickled her legs.

'What are you up to, Lucy?' whispered the person curled up next to her. 'You'd better not be thinkin' of leavin' without me.'

The person rolled over and revealed a cheeky looking girl, grinning in the gloom. Even in the half-light that was struggling through the window, Atlanta could see that the girl's face was streaked with dirt.

'Oh, no,' Atlanta replied, stalling for time while she worked out what she was supposed to say or do. 'I just needed to, er, stretch my legs.'

'Plenty of time for that later, eh?' chuckled the girl under her breath. Atlanta could hear other people stirring around the room.

'Keep the bloomin' noise down, Esther,' hissed a voice from a nearby bed. The girl next to her, who Atlanta reasoned must be the Esther in question, giggled mischievously.

Atlanta rolled onto her back and pushed herself up on her elbows, taking in as much as she could as the first glimmers of sunlight from outside began to brighten the room. She counted thirty beds, meaning there must be at least sixty girls sleeping in this bare room. Hanging directly above her, she noticed a bundle of leaves with small purple flowers. Lavender, she realised. Not much of an air freshener against the smell of dozens of sweaty children using chamber pots all night, Atlanta thought to herself, but maybe it was better than nothing.

She also noticed, with some alarm, that there didn't appear to be any way out. The walls were all solid apart from that large window. That mystery was solved almost immediately as a trapdoor banged open and a woman's head and shoulders appeared in the hatch.

'Up and at 'em, girls. The day's a-wasting!' she shouted.

'Yes, Mrs Timperley,' came the reply, from all the beds. Within moments, the room was a hive of activity, as girls sprang from their beds, all wearing the same plain, once-white dresses. Atlanta followed suit, with her bed-mate Esther close behind. Blankets were quickly straightened and a few miserable looking souls began collecting the chamber pots to be emptied.

The girls trooped down a rickety wooden ladder, through dark corridors and down steep steps into a stone-floored room. Here they were joined by a smaller group of boys, who had traipsed down from a separate bedroom, and together they began putting on wooden clogs, aprons and waistcoats. Mrs Timperley watched over them, hurrying those she felt weren't moving fast enough. She was a short woman with stocky arms, a ruddy complexion and the air of someone constantly in between a dozen important jobs.

Atlanta followed along with everyone else, keeping a close eye on Esther for clues as to what she should be doing. None of the children, she noticed, had changed out of the clothes they slept in. Nor, she realised had any of them washed, or brushed their teeth. In the light of day they were a sickly bunch with lean, skinny bodies and pale faces. Many of them were coughing. Not the sort of small cough you do to clear your throat when you wake up, but big, chesty, wracking coughs that shook their little bodies from head to toe.

Amongst the crowd, Atlanta noticed one boy, standing near to her. While the others were getting ready, he was taking a long time fiddling with his clogs, trying to look busy but not doing a very good job of it. Atlanta recognised the tactic from some of the boys at school, who would spend as much of the lesson as possible moving pens and paper around on the desk without ever actually getting their work done. This boy didn't seem to be slacking off out of naughtiness, but out of fear. He cowered away from Atlanta like a wounded animal, his head and shoulders naturally hunched, expecting life to rain blows down upon him. In a strange sort of way, it was nice to see someone as confused and worried as she felt. Atlanta tried to give him a reassuring smile.

Suddenly, a booming voice rang out, echoing off the stone floor. 'Samuel!' it bellowed, making the small, cringing boy jolt as if electricity had run through him. The shout had come from a tall, powerful looking man, who had just come in from the outside. His shirt sleeves were rolled up to the elbow, exposing hard rope-like muscles. Even though the sun was barely over the horizon, he was already sweating. From the way Mrs Timperely moved to stand at his side, arms folded sternly, Atlanta immediately pegged them as husband and wife.

'Come on, boy!' boomed Mr Timperley, but having already shocked the room into attention, the harsh edge had left his voice. He strode across the room, and he certainly didn't seem like someone you would want to make cross, but there was no cruelty in his manner. Mr Timperley put a firm, reassuring hand on Samuel's shoulder and gave him a fatherly pat, which nearly sent the feeble boy tumbling to the ground. As he staggered, Atlanta noticed that two of the fingers on Samuel's right hand were missing, the flesh around the knuckles forming a knot of twisted, dark- pink scar tissue. Atlanta couldn't help but gasp in horror. Samuel, meek and birdlike, quickly stuffed his injured hand inside his shirt and scurried away to join the line of children making their way outside.

The sun was already starting to warm the air. Atlanta, following in the line of children, stepped out of the house into a large garden. Unlike the gardens back home, there was no lawn, or decorative flowers and shrubs, here. This was a working garden, filled with rows of herbs and vegetables ready for the kitchen. As the children marched along the path towards a wooden gate, the Timperleys admired their crops. 'Cabbages look ready for harvest,' nodded Mr Timperley with satisfaction.

'Aye,' agreed his wife. 'There's pork at the shop. Lob scouse for supper.'

This caused a ripple of excitement among the children who were passing by. Atlanta didn't know what 'lob scouse' was, and thought it sounded quite horrible, but it was obviously a big treat. Even Samuel looked up, with what almost looked like excitement in his eyes, at the prospect.

'Poor Sam,' said Esther, who had quietly sidled up beside Atlanta as they filed through the garden.

'What happened to him?' asked Atlanta, unable to contain her curiosity.

'Same as happens to lots of us,' replied Esther, matter-of-factly. 'Got hisself caught up in the machine and it pulled his fingers clean off. Doctor patched 'im up, waited for it to heal, and now he's back at work.' Esther gave a shrug, as if this was the most normal thing in the world. 'Oh, that reminds me,' she added, pressing a small cloth bonnet into Atlanta's hand. 'You forgot this. Keep your hair tied up. Don't want to lose your head!' Esther chuckled at her dark joke, but Atlanta shuddered. What sort of place was this?

The line of children was now walking along a country lane that curved gently downwards. In the distance, Atlanta could hear a noise. A pulsing, throbbing noise that seemed to sit underneath the world itself. *THRUM, THRUM, THRUM*. It was both thrilling and scary. Weirdly, Atlanta found herself remembering a school trip to Alton Towers a few years earlier. There, the children had been lining up for a roller coaster that was hidden away inside a giant dome. All that could be heard was the thunder of the cars hurtling around the tracks, promising terror and excitement in one giddy package.

But this wasn't a roller coaster and these children weren't here for fun. Through the trees, Atlanta could see glimpses of a large building. *THRUM, THRUM, THRUM.* The noise grew louder and louder until it felt as if it filled the air around her. *THRUM, THRUM, THRUM.* They were there. The mill towered over the children. It was time to go to work.

CHAPTER 6

The Machine Orchestra

The mill filled Atlanta's vision. It stretched above her, with row upon row of windows filling the walls, and it stretched away from her too, a huge oblong of brick and glass with hard angles and steep walls. This giant building sat at the bottom of sloping hills on all sides, as if it had dropped from the sky and dented the earth as it landed with a crash.

Atlanta found it strangely familiar. Something about the mill had tickled a memory loose, and it now dashed and darted inside her brain while she struggled to grab hold of it. It was no use. The memory slipped away.

On the walk down from the house where the children all lived, Atlanta had noticed a river running behind the mill. That throbbing noise, she realised, must be a water wheel, constantly churning away to power the mill. At one end, a tall chimney was beginning to puff out gobs of black smoke, while in the middle a bell tower jabbed angrily at the morning sky. The bell began to ring and the sound made the children hurry inside.

If it was noisy outside, inside it was deafening. The endless pounding of the water wheel wasn't the only noise. There was another sound now, with its own rhythm, that grew louder as the children hurried down dark brick corridors, their clogs echoing as they jogged along. It was a rattling, clattering sound that rose and fell, the sound of the mill machinery lurching into life, ready for the working day.

Atlanta couldn't help but try to fit the sounds into a musical framework. It was something she did all the time, whether it was the rhythmic beep of a pedestrian crossing back home, or the gentle swoosh of the wind in the trees. Here, that gift was becoming a problem. The *thrum, thrum, thrum* of the water wheel joined with the clackety-clack of the machines until the noise seemed to be bursting from the walls themselves. Atlanta could feel it in her feet, the floors throbbing to this strange music. Yet try as she might, her imagination couldn't get this machine orchestra to play a tune. It was just noise, a thick smothering wall of jagged sound that hammered at her from all sides, its beats frustratingly out of time with each other. She was already getting a headache and the day had hardly begun.

Now the mill felt like some terrible beast, breathing heavily, its heart pulsing with immense power. They were walking into the belly of this beast, and a flutter of panic shivered in Atlanta's stomach at the thought. She quickly composed herself. She was, after all, a time traveller. She'd escaped down ancient passages, pursued by soldiers. She'd walked the streets of Manchester as bombs dropped in World War Two. Being scared of an old mill was silly.

The children had now emerged into a large, long room with windows down both sides. Dozens of machines were crammed into the space, tightly packed with little room for anyone to move between them. Each machine had a thick belt, which rose to the ceiling and looped around a spinning metal pole. It carried the motion provided by the water wheel throughout the mill. The air was thick with dust, thrown up by the raw cotton as it was unpacked and prepared. Even though the sun was still only just above the horizon, already the room was uncomfortably warm. Atlanta felt sick and woozy, the combination of nerves, her headache, the choking dust and itchy heat caught her off guard. She was also becoming hungry and wondered why none of these children had been given breakfast. Unaware that a girl from 2012 was in their midst, men and women were already at work, firing up the machines. They were hard-faced people, their arms sinewy and tough, but their legs and backs were bent and bowed from years spent stooped over these very same machines.

'Overlooker! Overlooker!' whispered one of the other children, as a stern looking man approached, clipboard in hand. The other children quickly kicked off their clogs, lined them neatly by the walls and scurried off into this dusty, pounding room barefoot. The man began ticking off names.

'Come on, slowcoach,' hissed Esther, grabbing the dazed Atlanta by the hand and dragging her into the thick of the machines. Atlanta suddenly realised that she had no idea what she was supposed to do, and this didn't look like the sort of place where putting your hand up and asking for help was a good idea. She decided to follow Esther's lead. She was the last to get going which earned her a hard stare from the overlooker. Esther pushed her towards one of the machines. It was made mostly of wood, and had thin strands of cotton threaded through it like a spider's web. A large wooden arm rattled up and down, pulling the cotton through until it was slowly woven into cloth. The noise was unbearable and dust drifted off the cotton constantly, each movement of the machine sent a fresh wave of particles into Atlanta's face. A sour-faced man operated the machine. He didn't even glance in her direction. He just kept his hands on the machine, eyes fixed on the clattering, moving parts.

'I'll see you later,' said Esther with a wink. 'Bonnet!' she added, scuttling off to crouch down under a machine a little further along the line. Atlanta gulped. She was alone, squatting with bare feet on a dusty, scratchy wooden floor, right next to a machine that she knew could snip off fingers and squash heads. The drive belt of the machine thundered around and around, only inches from her ear, and she suddenly realised what Esther had meant. She quickly tucked her hair up under her bonnet, before it could be caught in the belt and yank her, screaming, up into the machine.

Atlanta looked around to see what the other children were doing. Hunched, just like she was, they intently watched the threads of cotton on their machine. Every now and then, they would dart further under the machine, reach inside as the parts chomped and span, grab a piece of cotton that had split and then twist it back together. Atlanta was horrified. Was that what she was expected to do? The wooden arms of the machine now looked like gnashing teeth and the whirring reels like the spinning blades of her mum's food mixer. She didn't want to reach in there once, let alone spend the whole day doing it, over and over. An image of poor Sam and his missing fingers popped into her head and wouldn't go away.

She crouched and watched, dreading the moment when a thread would snap. She knew it would happen, but still held out hope that she'd get lucky and hers would be the only machine that ran perfectly all day. No sooner had she had this thought, than she saw a strand fray and split. She gulped in fear. Her fingers reached out. She could feel the whoosh of air from the machine's arms rattling back and forth, inches from her skin. 'Stop dawdlin', lass!' barked the man operating the machine.

Atlanta gritted her teeth and grabbed the two loose ends, forcing herself to ignore the slicing mechanisms to either side of her while she twisted the ends together. Once fixed, the thread was sucked back up into the machine and the man sent the shuttle on its way again. That was only the first time. The threads didn't break all the time, but often enough so that there was no chance to relax. Even when everything was running smoothly, Atlanta had to concentrate hard, staring at the spinning reels until her eyes hurt.

The day crawled along. She wasn't sure how long she'd been scrunched in between the machines, breathing in lungfuls of dust with the thumping din of the machine orchestra pounding in her ears, but it seemed like forever. She felt light-headed and dizzy, with the outside world growing hazy. A sudden tap on her shoulder startled her back into focus. It was an older girl, carrying a large metal pot in one hand and, in the other, a large spoon. On the spoon sat a thick glob of what looked like lumpy, grey clay. The girl rolled her eyes and thrust the spoon at Atlanta. Unsure of what to do, Atlanta quickly glanced at the other children and saw they were eating this gloopy paste out of their hands. The thought made her feel ill, but she cupped her hands like the others and let the girl dollop a sticky ball of mush onto her dusty fingers.

The room was at least quieter now, as everyone stopped work for, what Atlanta soon realised, was supposed to be breakfast. She sniffed the strange meal, warm and oozing in her dirty hands, and to her surprise it didn't smell too bad (once the scent had worked its way past the cotton fibres clogging her nostrils). She cautiously took a mouthful and discovered it was porridge. A thick, rather tasteless porridge with worrying bits of grit inside, but her stomach was growling and so Atlanta munched it all down, glad to have something stodgy and filling inside her at last.

No sooner had she finished than the clatter of the machines started again and the overlooker walked around, nudging workers back to their posts. Atlanta's hands were still sticky with porridge, but she knew there would be no warm sink to wash them clean. She rubbed them on her dress until the oats dried up and flaked off, and then she hurried back to work.

Though her stomach had stopped complaining, Atlanta now began to feel incredibly tired. She worked out that the children must have woken up at around five o'clock in the morning, and that it must now be around eight. For Atlanta, having travelled here from the afternoon in her time, it felt more like midnight and the strain was starting to show. The work was difficult, demanding intense concentration, and her muscles ached from having to crawl and crouch in such small spaces. The room was almost unbearably warm now and itchy, cotton fibres from the dust stuck to her sweating forehead.

She thought of her cosy bed back home, and of Lincoln, rolling around on the living-room carpet, watching cartoons without a care in the world. She imagined Geneva, off out with her friends, talking about clothes and pop stars at the shops. And she thought of her mum, folding washing, cleaning and cooking, always busy so they had somewhere nice to live. She looked around at these children working so hard for so little, with no parents to look after them, risking horrible injuries every minute of every day and never thinking it was unusual.

A wave of sadness suddenly crashed over her, churning up different emotions. She felt horribly alone and homesick, but also guilty for how much she took for granted, humbled that she couldn't even manage a few hours of the sort of work these children did all day, every day. She wanted to be back at home with friends, family and comfy furniture. She'd even rather be back in 1631 or 1940, in danger but filled with the thrill of adventure. If she'd been told one day earlier that the hardest thing she'd ever do as a time traveller was to work in a mill, she wouldn't have believed it. Now, she just wanted to get away. She considered reaching into her travel bag, pulling out her phone and hitting the emergency button, which would return her back to the present in an instant.

She thought about it, but she didn't do it. She

didn't want to let Mela down and she also felt a strange responsibility to the coughing, sickly children around her. If they could do it, with their skinny arms and wheezing lungs, why couldn't she? She vowed to work alongside them for as long she could, without complaint. It was the least she could do. Tears prickled at the corners of her eyes and the more she tried to blink them back, the faster they seemed to race to be first down her cheeks and onto the dusty floor of the mill.

A loud, cracking sound shook Atlanta out of her miserable daydream, closely followed by a sharp, stinging smack to the side of her head. She gasped in surprise more than pain. 'Oi!' barked the man who was working her machine. 'Now look what you've done!'

Atlanta followed his angry finger and saw that one of the reels had become tangled, which in turn had jammed the machine. The wooden frame creaked and shuddered as the scowling machinist shut it off before the whole thing splintered.

'Are you daft?' he bellowed, veins standing out on his temples. 'This'll put us right behind. Pay attention!'

This was too much for Atlanta and the quiet sobs

she'd been holding back suddenly exploded into a flood. The overlooker had heard the breakdown, followed by the tears, and came running over, expecting an accident. 'What's all this?' he demanded to know. By now, everything had stopped and people rushed over to see what had happened. Atlanta's cheeks burned red as the crowd gathered, and she could hear tuts and whispers when they discovered that, far from being injured, she was just crying next to a broken machine.

Esther emerged from the crowd and put an arm around Atlanta. 'Should I take her to see the doctor?' she asked the overlooker. He scoffed in return.

'Doctor? There's nowt wrong with her! It's Mr Greg she'll be seeing, so as he can decide what punishment she'll get for causing all this disruption! Get up, girl!'

With that, he roughly pulled Atlanta to her feet and marched her from the room. 'Get back to work,' he barked over his shoulder. Atlanta strained her neck to look around, and was just able to catch a glimpse of Esther's worried face. Then the door slammed shut behind her.

CHAPTER 7

The Honourable Mr Greg

The overlooker, still fuming, led Atlanta through the mill, past row upon row of machines all clattering away with men, women and children hard at work. A few eyes had turned in her direction as they passed, but most were too busy to pay attention to a young apprentice on her way to be told off.

Down some echoing stone stairs, the overlooker brought her to a wooden door. A polished brass panel screwed to the door, read 'R.H. Greg'. The overlooker straightened up, ran his fingers through his hair and tidied his shirt before knocking. There was no answer. The overlooker seemed flustered. He tried the door handle and it clicked open.

'Right,' he said, pushing Atlanta inside, 'you wait there for Mr Greg. I've got to go and tidy up your mess.' The door was pulled closed behind her and she heard angry footsteps retreating back into the mill.

Atlanta looked around. She was in a small, but well-decorated, room with a desk in the centre. Three large windows filled the room with sunlight, which bounced off the polished wood of the desk. A heavy, metal safe sat in one corner, squat and thick like a miniature castle, while an open fireplace almost covered one wall. Atlanta's bare toes scrunched and stretched on the warm rug under her feet.

Although the noise of the mill could still be heard, this room had clearly been carefully chosen for its location. What had been an overwhelming cacophony upstairs was reduced to a muffled thud here, allowing the rich, deep ticking of a clock on the mantelpiece to be heard. Even though she was in trouble, Atlanta couldn't help but relax a little. The room was so comfortable and calm, a reassuring cocoon, that she felt the panic and stress slipping away. There was only one chair, the one behind the desk, and she knew that sitting there would probably get her in even more trouble, so she remained standing. She closed her eyes and listened to the clock as it ticked off the seconds, in no particular hurry to mark the passing of the day.

Now that she had calmed down, the throb of her headache melted away. Atlanta always joked that she didn't need an iPod because she could fill her head with music at any time. Sometimes she would imagine scrolling through an imaginary list of her favourite tunes – a few pop songs but mostly classical music –

before selecting the one that best suited her mood. Other times, it was as if her brain was choosing for her, automatically picking the exact piece of music she needed to hear. Right now, she heard the first bars of Handel's Water Music, washing away the noise of the mill with their crisp, clean violins, the notes fluttering gently around her like butterflies.

'A fine piece of music indeed.'

Atlanta snapped to attention suddenly, startled by the man's voice behind her. She realised she had been humming along, out loud. She whirled around to see a man in a smart black coat and a white shirt with a high collar. This, clearly, was Mr Greg. He didn't look very old, maybe in his thirties, a few years older than Atlanta's mum. His hair was jet black and full, combed into a thick halo around his face, which was clean-shaven apart from bushy sideburns that stretched past his ears and down to his chin. He was studying Atlanta with an aloof stare, one eyebrow cocked in curiosity.

'Do you know what it is called?' Mr Greg asked. He walked past Atlanta and made his way to the desk. Atlanta cleared her throat nervously.

'Handel's Water Music, sir,' she replied, her voice reduced to a meek and timid mumble. 'The overture, to be exact.'

Mr Greg was now sat at his desk, hands clasped patiently in front of him. Atlanta thought she saw a brief flicker of a smile cross his lips. 'Quite correct,' Mr Greg nodded, approvingly. 'And quite remarkable. Tell me, where does an apprentice girl hear such music?'

Atlanta paused. The answer had sprung from her lips without thinking and only now she realised that in 1836 there were no radios, not even record players. Clearly, Lucy Garner, the girl whose life she had temporarily borrowed, was not the sort of girl to attend concerts 'I... I can't remember,' Atlanta said, bowing her head slightly. 'I just heard it somewhere and it stuck with me. It's such a beautiful piece of music. It always makes me think of summer.'

'Well, Lucy Garner, it seems there is more to you than meets the eye,' said Mr Greg, 'but it is not the joy and beauty of music that brings you before me today, is it?' His tone hardened as he spoke. 'What have you to say about your unfortunate lapse in concentration that has left one of my machines, my rather expensive machines on which we all rely for our livelihoods, out of service?'

'I'm really sorry,' Atlanta pleaded. 'The work was

so hard and I had a headache and, and I just couldn't...'
Her words trailed off as she realised how feeble her
excuses must sound. 'I'm sorry,' she repeated, her
voice barely a whisper. Mr Greg rose from his desk
and turned to the window, looking out over the countryside beyond. For agonising moments, he said nothing. The clock ticked on, its lazy rhythm now feeling
like the marking out of eternity. Atlanta fidgeted,
watching Mr Greg's back for clues to what might happen next. She was suddenly terrified that she would
be beaten or whipped. Wasn't that what they did?

'Please don't hit me!' she blurted out. At that, Mr
Greg turned back to face her. He looked angry, but
also slightly offended, Atlanta thought.

'I know you have not been here with us long,
Lucy Garner, but I would have thought that by now
you would know that we do not beat children here,'
he snapped. 'A cuff around the ear to keep your attention, certainly, but I do not hold with the practice of
physically punishing my workforce. You may have
heard such stories from other mills, but not here. Not
here.' He repeated the words as if it was a matter of
pride. As he spoke, he took a file from his desk drawer
and began leafing through it. With a flourish, he found
whatever he was looking for and plucked a sheet of

paper from the file. He walked around from behind the desk and stood in front of Atlanta, tilting his head from side to side as he studied her.

'Yes, the work is hard,' he continued, 'but that is the way of the world. A hard day's work is nothing to shirk from.' He handed the piece of paper to Atlanta. It appeared to be a contract of some kind, written in old-fashioned legal words that Atlanta could barely understand. In amongst the printed text there were gaps, and in these gaps she could see names and dates had been written by hand in heavy black ink. Lucy Garner was the name on this one.

'Your notice of indenture,' said Mr Greg. 'You remember this, I trust? It binds you to work for me until the age of eighteen years. In return, you are provided with a roof over your head, a bed to sleep in and clothes for your back, are you not?' Atlanta nodded, even though, of course, this was the first time anyone had explained the apprentice system to her.

'You are fed three times a day,' Mr Greg continued sternly, 'and your evening meal is not rationed. You are free to eat until you are full. This, I feel, is far preferable to the workhouses of Manchester where children are half-starved and forced to sleep on cold stone. Do you agree?' Atlanta nodded again. 'Furthermore, you are given several hours of school tuition every week, because I believe an educated child is a more useful child. And, should you become ill, you receive the attention of a most qualified doctor.'

At that, there was a knock at the door. 'Aah, speak of the devil,' smiled Mr Greg. 'Come in, Dr Holland,' he called out. The door swung open and in came a short, balding man with a small inquisitive face and a large, leather bag. He bustled in immediately, placed his bag on the desk and squinted at Atlanta, not taking his eyes off her even as he spoke to Mr Greg.

'Is this the girl?' Dr Holland asked, not even waiting for a reply before grabbing Atlanta by the chin and peering into her mouth.

'She broke down in hysterics in the machine room,' said Mr Greg. Dr Holland nodded knowingly.

'Yes, yes,' he said, jabbing a finger into Atlanta's tummy, making her wince. 'Very common in girls and womenfolk.' The doctor turned his attention from Atlanta, as if she wasn't even there any more, and spoke directly to Mr Greg. Atlanta thought he was very rude. 'Probably not been eating enough, staying up too late gossiping. It leads to an excess of black bile, which in turn causes this melancholy.' Atlanta thought this sounded like a load of old rubbish, not like a real doctor at all, but she dared not say anything. The doctor opened his bag and began removing jars and bottles. Atlanta noticed one had the word 'leeches' written on the side. She swallowed hard and hoped he didn't reach for that one. To her relief, he kept searching in his bag, finally removing a small cloth bundle, tied with string. 'Send her back to the apprentice house and ask Mrs Timperley to brew this in some hot water. That should reduce the bile and restore her to normal. I would keep her away from the machines for the rest of today, however.'

Mr Greg sighed. 'Very well, if you insist,' he said, looking annoyed. He turned to Atlanta with a frown. 'Young lady,' he said in a low and calm voice. Atlanta knew from watching other children being told off by teachers at school that this meant he was about to deliver his final verdict on her misbehaviour. 'You will be fined the exact cost of the repairs to the machine and will work whatever extra hours are required to make up that difference. Do I make myself clear?'

Atlanta nodded. 'Yes sir,' she mumbled, secretly rather happy that she wouldn't have to go back to that awful, noisy room.

'Dr Holland will be walking past the apprentice house when he goes,' continued Mr Greg. 'You will go with him, and inform Mrs Timperley that you are to assist her for the rest of the day in whatever chores she may require. Tomorrow, you will return to work as normal and we shall have no repeat of today's unfortunate incident. I trust I make myself clear.'

With that, Mr Greg turned his attention back to his desk, where he opened a large leather-bound book and began filling lots of tiny columns with numbers. The meeting, it seemed, was over.

'Come on, girl,' said Dr Holland. He packed away his things and Atlanta followed him out of the door.

CHAPTER 8

Esther's Plan

Atlanta left Mr Greg's office with mixed feelings. Knowing she wouldn't be going back into the mill, squatting under those terrible machines with their clattering hammering in her ears, came as a huge relief. But at the same time, she felt sad and guilty that she hadn't even managed to last a whole morning, while the other children would be there all day, for years to come. It made her feel like a failure, a soft and spoiled weakling, and she didn't like it.

Dr Holland waited outside the mill while Atlanta hurried inside to get her shoes. She kept her head down, cheeks burning with shame, as she scuttled past the machines. She was sure everyone was staring and whispering about her. Out of the corner of her eye, she saw young Sam, who gave her a sympathetic smile. That made her feel worse. Sam looked like he weighed as much as a piece of string; one of his hands had been chopped and mangled, yet he was able to work harder and longer than Atlanta. When Atlanta reached the corner where the apprentices left their clogs, she heard a hiss. 'Psssst!' Atlanta turned around and saw Esther, who had scurried away from her machine to see her. Esther gave Atlanta a quick hug and whispered in her ear.

'Don't worry,' she said. 'It'll never happen again, right? I'll see you tonight. Nowt'll change our plans.'

'Oi! Get back over here!' shouted the overlooker, who had spotted Esther's disobedient break. Esther winked once and ran back to her machine. Atlanta was dazed. What plan? What was Esther talking about? The overlooker, satisfied that Esther was back at work, threw a scowl in Atlanta's direction, just to remind her that her mistake had not been forgotten. Atlanta blushed bright red again and, quickly slipping her feet into the hard wooden clogs, dashed outside, clip-clopping as she went. Outside, Dr Holland was looking at his pocket watch impatiently.

'Make haste, girl!' he snapped. 'I have patients to see and must be in Knutsford by noon.' He strode off up the hill towards the apprentice house, with Atlanta trailing close behind.

The doctor didn't seem interested in conversation, apart from an occasional 'harrumph' noise that was directed at nobody in particular. Soon, the mill with its terrible noise, was receding behind them and the scenery was becoming more comforting. The air was clean and sweet, and there was a natural, earthy smell. Birds twittered and chirruped overhead, while red squirrels darted and dashed across the path ahead of them. How could a place be so horrible and so beautiful at the same time, wondered Atlanta. After a few more minutes, they had reached the top of the hill and the apprentice house popped into view, a squat, white cube against the deep blue sky. To her left, over the fields, she could see a small huddle of other houses. She hadn't noticed them in the half-light during the dawn march to the mill.

'What's that place?' she asked Dr Holland. He stopped and squinted at her curiously, just as he had in Mr Greg's office. It was as if she was a problem to be solved rather than a person, Atlanta thought.

'Are you mocking me, girl?' asked the doctor. Atlanta realised that, as Lucy Garner, the answer to her question should have been obvious.

'Oh, I forgot, sir,' she replied, putting on a bit of an act. 'What with all the...' She struggled to remember the word the doctor had used, then it came to her, 'melancholy,' she finished. 'The melancholy has made me forgetful.'

The doctor studied her a moment longer and,

convinced she was not teasing him, replied, 'That is the village of Styal,' a touch pompously, 'where the mill workers and their families – those that have families – live, at Mr Greg's convenience, as well you know.'

Atlanta nodded politely. By now they had reached the wooden gate of the apprentice house and Mr Timperley, who was still working in the gardens, came to meet them.

'Now, now,' he said sternly, 'what's this then?' Dr Holland explained the situation, and Atlanta squirmed underneath Mr Timperley's stare as the details of her accident were spelled out.

His duty completed, Dr Holland nodded curtly to Mr Timperley and carried on his way up the lane. Once he was out of view, Mr Timperley turned his attention to Atlanta.

'Not havin' a very good day, are you?' he said, his expression unreadable.

'No, sir,' muttered Atlanta.

Mr Timperley placed a large, rough hand on her shoulder and ushered her into the garden. 'Come on,' he said, with a small hint of affection in his voice, 'the wife'll see you right.' Inside the house was quiet compared to the chaos of the morning. Mrs Timperley was bustling around, with large pots of boiling water on a stove in the corner and piles of vegetables lined up on the wooden table in the centre. She looked up as Atlanta and Mr Timperley entered, and listened intently as the story of Atlanta's breakdown at the machine was relayed once more.

'Well then,' she said, clapping her hands together in a brisk, busy manner, 'let's see if we can't keep you busy, and let's hope you don't break owt in here.' Mrs Timperley put Atlanta to work washing the vegetables that Mr Timperley had brought in from the garden. Atlanta scrubbed them in a cold basin, until the water turned muddy, and then she was sent outside to pour the water away and refill the basin from a hand pump. It was hard work, but nothing compared to what she had experienced in the mill. Clearly, Mrs Timperley was happy for the company as well. Her stern manner soon gave way to a cheery, chatty nature. It didn't seem that Atlanta was required to join in the conversation, so she simply kept busy, moving on to carefully chop the carrots and potatoes once they were clean. All the while, Mrs Timperley talked on and on about what was happening in the village.

Once the vegetables had been boiled in a large pot, they were added to the porridge of the morning, and Mrs Timperley watched while Atlanta stirred the gloopy mixture with a large spoon. This, Atlanta discovered, would be the lunch for the mill workers. Mrs Timperley decided it was best if Atlanta didn't go back to the mill, so she gave her a handful of the porridge and set off to deliver it herself.

When Mrs Timperley returned, Mr Timperley came in from the garden and together they took their lunch of bread, cheese and fruit in the sitting room. Although not as polished and comfortable as Mr Greg's office, it still had nice furniture and a rug on the floor. Atlanta wasn't allowed in and had to wait at the door while the couple decided what else she could do. Mr Timperley decided she was to sit in the school room – a large, chilly room with benches and white walls – and practice her alphabet. Sitting on a hard wooden bench, Atlanta found that there was no paper. Instead, she was expected to write with her finger in a tray of sand. Of course, since Atlanta had been going to school since she was a five-year-old, writing was no problem at all, so she quickly scribbled some letters in the sand and then went to look out of the window. All she could see over the rows of vegetables, and past a tatty scarecrow, were fields, trees and blue skies. The mill was hidden from view at the bottom of the valley, so the only buildings in sight were the rooftops of Styal Village, just visible through the trees if she craned her neck.

'Daydreaming, are we?' came Mr Timperley's voice. Atlanta turned in surprise. He was looking at her disapprovingly. 'I suppose you think the view from the window is more important than practicing your... Oh.' Mr Timperley stopped as he noticed the sand tray covered with letters. 'That's not bad at all,' he admitted. 'Maybe you're learning summat after all,' he added with a wink. Atlanta stifled a giggle. If she wasn't careful, people would start thinking Lucy Garner was a genius, at least by nineteenth century standards. They didn't know she had help from a girl who wouldn't be born for almost two hundred years! The afternoon passed in a blur of more jobs. There seemed to be no end to the things that needed doing, and it was clear that Mrs Timperley was quietly pleased to have someone else to tackle them with her. They swept, cleaned and tidied, and then began preparing the evening meal of lob scouse. Atlanta was disappointed to discover this strange sounding meal was nothing more than a vegetable broth with pork. Of course, her rumbling tummy reminded her that after a day of hard work and only two handfuls of porridge, it would definitely be a real treat.

With the broth bubbling in the pot, Mrs Timperley led Atlanta outside. The sun was now starting to dip down towards the horizon and the hot summer air was cooling. Mrs Timperley gave Atlanta an approving pat on the head. 'I'll be sure to tell Mr Greg how hard you worked today,' she said. 'I've finished nice and early thanks to your help, and I think we both deserve a rest.' They sat down on a rickety wooden bench and watched Mr Timperley in comfortable silence while he tugged weeds out from one of the vegetable patches.

Before long the sound of footsteps could be heard coming up the hill as the mill emptied out. A crowd of people reached the corner of the apprentice house garden. The men and women, and a few children, continued down a footpath running alongside the far hedge as they made their way back to the cottages in Styal. Some of the men nodded a greeting to Mr Timperley who nodded back. Everyone seemed too exhausted for chatter. Atlanta, from her bench, couldn't help but think of the end of the school day back home, when kids would pour out into the street in a fizz of excitement. Here, the children trudged, aching fingers blistered and lungs filled with dust.

The apprentices poured through the garden gate like a stream of dirty water. Mrs Timperley rose to greet them. 'Come on, come on!' she bustled, hurrying them through the garden and into the house. Some of them shot Atlanta sour glances. She realised that the sight of her sitting out in the garden while they'd been working for over twelve hours made her look very lazy. She wanted to stop them and explain, but decided against it. They had a right to be annoyed. She got to her feet and joined the line at the back. Maybe, when everyone was gratefully gulping down their lob scouse, Mrs Timperley would tell the children how Atlanta had helped to make it and they'd all change their minds. It was a nice idea, but she doubted it would happen that way. The line of tired children snaked past the wall that separated the garden from the sheds and outhouses and then went in by the back door.

'Pssst!' That whisper again. Atlanta looked around, she knew it was Esther, but where was she? 'Over here!' hissed the voice again. Atlanta peered in the direction of the sound, but the sun was now low on the horizon casting long shadows over the garden. 'Here, silly!'

Now Atlanta spotted her, Esther's unmistakable cheeky grin, framed by a mop of straw-coloured hair was peeping out from behind the wall. Atlanta looked around uncertainly. The children were almost all in the house now and there was a large gap opening up ahead of Atlanta in the line. She had to go in, but suddenly Esther lunged out from her hiding place, grabbed at Atlanta's arm and dragged her away from the line.

'Now's our chance!' whispered Esther, excitement bubbling in her voice.

'Chance for what?' Atlanta hissed in return. 'We need to get inside or we'll be in trouble.' Esther looked at her, suspiciously.

'Our chance to get away from here, you daft sod,' she said. 'Away from this bloody mill, and porridge, and machines that chop off fingers.' Atlanta's stomach did queasy somersaults as the penny dropped. They were running away. This was the plan Esther had mentioned.

'Now, while everyone is busy stuffing their faces!' Esther said, and with that she was off in a running crouch towards the fence at the back of the house. She scrambled over it and waved for Atlanta to follow. Atlanta was frozen. She understood exactly why Esther – and, she supposed, Lucy – wanted to run away from the mill. She couldn't even face a full day in there, never mind a lifetime. But she was also worried. Was it fair for her to get Lucy into trouble? What if the girls got lost, or ended up somewhere worse? Atlanta was never more aware that, on her travels, she wasn't really Atlanta any more. She had borrowed somebody else's life, and might be about to ruin it forever. But, she reasoned, from the way Esther was talking, it sounded like this was Lucy's plan as well. What if this was supposed to happen? All the children were now inside the house.

It wouldn't take long for the Timperleys to notice two of the girls were missing. Atlanta made up her mind and dashed to the fence, climbing over it in a flash.

'Let's go!' laughed Esther, racing into the darkening countryside. Atlanta gulped down her fear and followed.

CHAPTER 9

Time Stream Error

Atlanta could barely keep sight of Esther who was running on ahead. The girls were now in a thick wooded area, and the last rays of sunlight struggled to pierce the gloom. Atlanta's sides ached and her breath was hot and scratchy, but she kept running, her fear of being left behind greater than her worry that she might trip on some unseen root or stone.

Eventually, Esther slowed down and stopped. Atlanta staggered to a halt beside her. Neither spoke for several minutes, instead collapsing to the ground and leaning back on a large oak tree while they gasped for breath, their burning lungs cooled by the evening air. Atlanta had been listening out for any sound of pursuit, but apart from what sounded like a faint shout in the distance, several minutes earlier, it seemed they had made it away without being followed. The girls looked at each other and their wheezes turned to laughs.

'Right,' said Esther, getting her breath back. 'Let's find a farm and sleep in a barn tonight. First thing in the morning we can look for the road, and follow it to town. From there, we'll...' She paused, awkwardly. 'Well, from there we'll work out what to do next. Maybe try to get to Manchester and then sneak on a train from there.'

Atlanta sighed. It was clear Esther had no idea what to do next, and Atlanta wouldn't be able to help for much longer. Just then, she felt an urgent buzzing from her travel bag, still stuck firmly to the swimming costume beneath her clothes. Her phone! It must be time to return, but there was no way to do that while Esther was watching.

'I'm just going to have a look around,' Atlanta said, getting to her feet and pressing her hand over the buzzing phone to muffle the noise. Before Esther could say anything she'd disappeared deeper into the trees. Once Atlanta was satisfied that Esther hadn't followed her, she reached inside her clothes and pulled her phone out from the pouch. There was an unexpected message on the screen.

‹Endrant Command›
Boson field stability 36% and falling
Quantum lock disengaged
system error

The buzzing from the phone was getting stronger, until it was stinging Atlanta's hand just holding onto it. She looked at the message, trying to work out what it meant. Cautiously she pressed a few keys, but nothing happened. Panic began to bite and scratch at her thoughts. Was she stuck here? How could she contact Mela? Then the screen changed.

‹Endrant Command›
Boson field stability failure
Emergency protocol inactive
Timestream System::Void button1_Click(System::Object^ sender, System::EventArgs^ e)
∑ 15799(Location.X,Location.Y,Location.Z,0,0,0,Date,,,0);
system error

The screen filled with gibberish and meaningless symbols. Now Atlanta began frantically pressing every button. No response. She could hear the whining sound that came with every trip through time, but it sounded different. It was always a high C note, but now it was wobbling, up and down like a siren. It grew louder and louder until it filled Atlanta's head. Then... Nothing.

Atlanta opened her eyes and her heart sank; this wasn't her house! They had not got her back home. She was still outside, in the country, but now it was daylight. She was standing by a cobbled lane, which curved away along the horizon to her left and down a hill to her right. She turned and looked around behind her. A stone signpost poked out from the bottom of a bramble hedge, claiming Derby was forty miles in the direction of the hill. Atlanta was really scared now. She was alone and lost with no idea where, or when she was! Suddenly, she heard whistling coming from up the hill. She quickly tucked the phone back inside her clothes. When she saw Esther's yellow mop of hair coming towards her, Atlanta had to resist the urge to run over and give her a hug.

'I got some apples from that wagon,' said Esther, as if carrying on a conversation that Atlanta had missed, 'and a few crusts of bread.'

Atlanta looked at her friend. If she had been dirty and scruffy back at the mill, she was even worse now. Her dress was streaked with mud, her skin was even paler than before and her eyes had lost some of their cheeky sparkle. It must mean that she herself had been pulled forwards in time, but for how long? A few hours? A day? Or more?

Her hand trembling, Atlanta reached out for one of the apples. She was starving. She sank her teeth into it gratefully. The sweet, juicy flesh of the fruit seemed like the best thing she'd ever tasted. Esther was chewing on a crust of bread, looking ahead down the road.

'We'll keep walking until sunset,' Esther mumbled through the crumbs. 'There are lots of farms this way, so we should find somewhere to sleep.' She finished her food without saying another word and then got up and started walking down the hill, not even turning to see if her friend was following.

Atlanta was about to say something, but then the whining noise came back, softly at first but growing louder all the time. Atlanta screwed her eyes closed. The noise got louder, until it felt like her head must surely burst. Then... Nothing.

Atlanta cautiously opened her eyes a second time. Darkness. Complete and total darkness. She swayed unsteadily; the repeated trips were leaving her horribly dizzy. For a moment, she feared that she had been pulled out of time and space and left in some empty void, but she refused to panic. 'Pull yourself together!' she scolded herself, and was surprised to hear her words out loud, echoing off nearby surfaces. With something real to cling to, Atlanta quickly made sense of her surroundings. The floor beneath her was hard rough wood. Still on her knees, she inched around until her fingers brushed a cold brick wall. She shuffled along it, trying to measure it in her head. Wherever she was, it was a small room, with a door in one wall. There was a pile of straw in a corner, and a stale sweaty smell. At one point, her exploring fingertips brushed against what felt like a bowl. She investigated it carefully, bringing it up to her face in the hope of sensing some clue to her location.

Porridge. It smelled of porridge. She was back at the apprentice house, she was sure of it. She felt for the door knob and rattled it, but it wouldn't budge. She was locked in. Was she in one of the sheds? Was this Lucy's punishment for running away? Atlanta had no idea how much time had passed since Esther had walked away from her in the country, or how long she'd been here in this locked room.

'Hello?' she shouted, banging on the door. She pressed her ear against it, but could hear nothing from outside. For all she knew it could be the middle of the night, or the middle of the day. Maybe it wasn't the apprentice house at all, but some lonely room buried deep in the mill, where nobody would check on her. She knocked again, more urgently. 'Help!' she cried, although she knew that if Lucy had been locked in this room on purpose, there wasn't much chance of being let out just because she asked.

'Keep the noise down!' came a voice from outside, accompanied by heavy footsteps on the floor. Atlanta recognised the deep tone of the voice. It was Mr Timperley.

'Please let me out,' she pleaded, her voice cracking as she held back her tears. 'I want to go home.' She wasn't even trying to pretend to be Lucy now. She was just Atlanta, and more than anything she wanted to be back in Moss Side, in 2012, with her mum, Geneva and Lincoln.

'This is your home. And you'll stay put until Mr Greg says otherwise,' Mr Timperley's voice was now close to the door. 'I'm sorry, girl, but that's how it has to be. There's none round here that'll go against Mr Greg's orders on this matter, harsh as it may be.' He was no longer shouting, but talking normally, even a little quietly, as if he didn't want to be overheard. 'What were you thinking, Lucy? Running away like that?'

'What about Esther?' Atlanta asked, through the

door. 'Did she come back as well?'

'No,' said Mr Timperley, softly. 'No sign of her yet. Least not in the two days since you turned up again. Bide your time, lass. Make amends for what you did and we'll see you right.'

Mr Timperley's footsteps retreated from the door and Atlanta was left alone once again. Two days, she thought. Poor Lucy had been in this dark room for two whole days. The very thought chilled her to the bone, especially since she might be in there just as long, if not longer. Now that she desperately needed it most, the unmistakable whine of the time stream, wasn't putting in an appearance. Atlanta shuffled to the back wall of her cell and sat down, her back against the rough brick. She sighed and tried not to think of home.

Hours passed, or it might have been minutes. With no light, there was no way to know. All Atlanta did know was that she hadn't slept since she began this journey, and with nothing else to do, she began to doze. She'd barely dropped off when she was jerked awake again. There was a slight pulse coming from her phone. She pulled it out and held it in her hands, waiting to see if it would pulse again. It did. Then it gave a long buzz and suddenly the screen burst into life, dazzling Atlanta after so long staring into the blackness. A message scrolled up the screen.

‹Remote System Reboot›
Code operative 15799 located
Emergency retrieval plan initiated
...
‹Attempting Subspace Contact›
...

Atlanta's heart soared. She didn't understand the technical words but the intention was clear: Mela had found her and was going to get her home. The screen cleared and another message appeared.

Atlanta,

It's Mela. Thank goodness we have found you. You've been caught in a tachyon slip, drifting through time, and we had to scan each time quadrant to pin you down.

First of all - don't panic! I'm coming to get you. We need to pull you to new coordinates where we can extract you. In order to make sure you're out of the slip, we'll need to shunt you a few years ahead and into a new identity. This may be confusing and strange but hang in there and keep your wits about you. I'll see you

soon. Enter your code to confirm you are OK and we'll get you out.
Mela

Atlanta quickly keyed in 15799 and pressed the green button. Almost immediately the phone buzzed three times, one after another, and the high-pitched whining sound rushed in around her. Atlanta curled into a ball, closed her eyes, and hoped that nothing would go wrong this time. The noise built to fever pitch and then, once again... Nothing.

CHAPTER 10

Living In Styal Village

Even before she opened her eyes, Atlanta knew she was out of that dark room. Light crept in through her eyelids and she eagerly looked around, glad to see sunlight again. She was back in the mill, but something was different. There was nobody around; the machines stood motionless and silent. Even with the sunshine outside, it was rather creepy, as if all the people had suddenly vanished. Her phone buzzed again. Another message.

> Take off the clothes you are wearing and leave them in the room. There are new clothes in corner. They are boy's clothes – sorry! Come to churchyard in village. Year is 1863.

The urgent tone of the message spurred Atlanta into action. She was still wearing Lucy's dress from 1836, twenty-seven years before! She spotted the pile of boy's clothes tucked away in one corner of the room, and quickly got changed. She made her way out of the now silent machine room, walking past row upon row of eerily abandoned looms, tiptoeing cautiously down the stairs and into the yard outside the mill. Here, at least, there were other people, but far fewer than she expected. A group of men were working on a wall, and further down some more were fixing a gate. Two women were carrying some rolls of cloth, but this was not the bustling noisy place she'd visited before.

'Oi! What you doin' in there, you little blighter?' One of the men had spotted Atlanta creeping out of the mill. 'Mr Greg'll 'ave your hide if he catches you sniffin' around in there!'

Atlanta bolted up the hill towards the apprentice house. Knowing that she, as Lucy, had been locked inside one of the sheds there, only minutes ago for her, but almost thirty years ago in reality, was very weird. But, there was no time to think about such things now. She needed to get to the churchyard at Styal, as quickly as possible. As she entered the tiny village, Atlanta couldn't help noticing that the cottages were arranged in neat rows, just like the machines in the mill. They were small but charming, and a little shop was in the centre. It almost looked like toy town, but the sad faces on the women and children didn't suit the playful image. Eager to find out what was going on, and why the mill had stopped running, Atlanta sidled over to a pair of gossiping women and listened in.

'I've heard tell that Mr Greg only has enough cotton left for another two months,' said one woman, her hair tucked up inside a spotted blue scarf tied around her head. She tutted and clucked with the confidence of someone who was sure they had all the facts and would stand for no contradictions.

'Happen that's not what Esther says,' replied the other woman, dismissively. Atlanta froze. Esther was here?

'Esther Price don't know owt about nowt,' scoffed the first lady, folding her arms as if to say the argument ended there. 'There's no cotton comin' in, and Mr Greg's supply'll only last so long, you mark my words. We'll be as hungry as the rest by Christmas.'

Atlanta couldn't hold her tongue any longer. 'Is Esther at the apprentice house?' she asked.

'Now what would she be doing there?' asked the scowling woman with the headscarf. 'There's been no apprentices here for over ten year. She's at home, here in the village, and what business is it of yours?'

Atlanta thought fast. She was supposed to be going to the church to be brought home, and she didn't want to risk being stranded here, but at the same time she really needed to see Esther and find out what had happened to her and Lucy.

'I've got a message for her,' Atlanta fibbed, rather convincingly she thought. 'A message from the shop,' she added, for extra effect. It seemed to work, because the woman snorted and nodded in the direction of a house in the middle of a row opposite. 'Number four,' she said, grudgingly.

Atlanta hurried over to the house and knocked nervously at the door. A woman answered, her hands covered in flour and crumbs. 'Who are you then?' she asked, a familiar twinkle in her eye. Atlanta looked at Esther in disbelief. Only a few hours ago, she'd left Esther Price in a barn in the 1830s, a friend her own age. Now here she was, a middle-aged woman. Time travel could tie your brain in some very confusing knots.

'Esther!' she cried, forgetting that to Esther's eyes the person at the door was a young boy. 'I mean, I'm...er... er,' she struggled to think of a clever explanation of who she was, but decided to go with something close to the truth. 'I'm a friend of Lucy Garner's,' she said.

Esther's eyebrows crawled up her forehead in surprise. 'Well,' she said, 'you'd better come in.'

Inside the house was cosy, but bare. The furniture was hard and wooden, and a threadbare rug was the closest there was to any decoration. It wasn't comfortable, Atlanta thought, but it was strangely comforting. An honest, simple home.

'Take a seat,' Esther insisted, offering a plate of hard, oaty biscuits. Atlanta took one and nibbled at it. 'So what can I do for you, young master friend-of-Lucy?' Esther continued, with a smile.

'I just...I mean, she just wanted to know how you were,' stammered Atlanta. 'You ran away together, didn't you?'

'Aye,' smiled Esther, her eyes glazing over as they drifted to some far away memory. 'We did. And we caught merry hell for it after. Mr Greg wanted to cut our hair off, so they say, but the law wouldn't allow it. So he locked us up in the shed at the apprentice house for the same number of days we were gone. Lucy got four, I got ten.'

'But you're still here?' Atlanta asked, surprised. 'Why didn't you leave when you were old enough?'

'Mr Greg may be a stiff old boot,' Esther explained, 'but he's not so bad, all things considered. He's a smart one too. Stocked up on raw cotton before the war in the Americas put a stop to raw cotton coming into England. The mill only runs a few days a week now, but it's still going, which is more than you can say for most. I've heard tell there's folk starving in the street in Lancashire, and the same'll happen here once Mr Greg's supply runs out.'

Atlanta couldn't believe what she was hearing. A war in America? People starving to death in England? 'What about the apprentices?' she asked. Esther looked at her curiously.

'There's been no apprentices in almost twenty years,' she said, 'as well you'd know. All manner of safety and factory laws made it so it were more trouble than it were worth to have children work the mills.'

Knowing that no more children were working under those horrible, clattering machines made Atlanta happy, but also strangely sad. She wondered what had happened to all the other children who had lived and worked with Lucy and Esther.

'How is Lucy?' Esther asked, her voice suddenly soft and sad. 'She moved away and we lost touch. I always worried that she blamed me for what happened.'

'Oh, she's fine,' Atlanta lied, now feeling rather guilty for her fib. 'She's living in Derbyshire,' she added, remembering the signpost from their journey.

'That's good,' nodded Esther. 'And you are?'

'Oh, I'm, er, John. Her... her nephew,' Atlanta replied. She munched on her biscuit, awkwardly. 'Well, you be sure to tell Lucy I asked after her,' Esther said briskly as she rose and dusted her hands on her apron. 'It was nice to meet you, John,' she added with a wink. Atlanta didn't bother to hide her smile. Everything had turned out OK for Esther, and now she could leave for home with a clear conscience. Esther walked her to the door and waved her off. Atlanta gave her one last beaming smile and headed for the large church at the other side of the village.

The churchyard was cramped and slightly gloomy, framed by tall trees and hedges. Gravestones poked from the ground like crooked teeth, but it felt peaceful rather than spooky.

A girl came hurrying out from around the back of the church. With relief she saw that it was Mela.

'Atlanta! I'm so sorry! So, so sorry! We're still trying to work out what went wrong, but at least we've got you now. Was it very scary, being tugged around in time and space?'

'Yeah! It was,' Atlanta said slowly. 'I didn't know what was going on, or where, or when, I was. I thought maybe I'd be lost forever.'

'Never,' insisted Mela. 'We've never lost a traveller, and we're not going to start now. That's why I've come to bring you back personally. It requires very careful calculations, but it means that we can be sure to bring you home safely. And,' Mela added, whispering excitedly, 'it's fun to do a trip myself. We're only supposed to jump back to make primary contact, like when we met at the museum for the first time, and it's only been in the last few months that they've been able to send us back this far. I've not had much time to look around, of course, but even so I can feel how different it is even to your time. Tell me, what are these stone markers?'

'Those are graves. It's to show where dead people are buried,' explained Atlanta, and then giggled at the look of horror and disgust on Mela's face. She sometimes forgot that for all her complicated science talk, Mela had a very limited understanding of what normal life was like in the past.

'Are you ready to leave?' Mela asked.

'Oh, yes please,' Atlanta said, quickly taking off the boy's clothes so that she was only wearing her swimming costume. Mela took out a device that looked a bit like Atlanta's modified phone, but smaller and seemingly made from clear glass or plastic. Mela's six fingers danced across an invisible keypad and then made a swooping motion across and down the device.

'Time to go home,' she smiled, as she took Atlanta's hand.

The high-pitched whine that had almost driven Atlanta crazy with fear and worry before, now felt like a welcome relief. Atlanta closed her eyes and let it rush up to meet her. The noise surrounded her and then... Nothing.

CHAPTER 11

Landing Back Home
And A Flight Out

Atlanta found herself surrounded by leaves and branches. Her heart sank at the thought of being bounced around the countryside in the nineteenth century again, but then she heard the unmistakable growl of a car driving past. She pushed her way through the branches and discovered she wasn't in the countryside at all, but in the middle of a cluster of trees on a roundabout in the middle of a main road. In fact, she knew exactly where she was: her house was just around the corner!

She waited for a gap in the traffic then darted across to the pavement, uncomfortably aware that she was wearing only a swimming costume. Luckily, it was the height of summer so such attire wasn't completely out of the ordinary, but she still felt self-conscious running down the street in bare feet. As she entered her own road and saw her house in the distance, Atlanta's pace quickened. She desperately wanted to get inside, hug her mum and get some proper food. It was only when she reached the front door that she realised she didn't have her keys. She didn't have anything, apart from her phone. She knocked on the door and it opened almost immediately. Simon, her best friend, was standing in the hallway, his eyes like saucers.

'Atlanta!' he gasped.

'She's here! She's here!' he called back into the house. The hall filled with people – Geneva, her nana Prestwich, Lincoln in his pyjamas, even some of the neighbours. At the front, looking both furious and relieved at the same time, was her mum.

'Where have you been?' she scolded, but her anger vanished almost instantly and she pulled Atlanta into a breathless squeeze of a hug. Her hands were shaking. 'Are you OK? Did anything happen? Are you OK?' she babbled.

'I'm fine, Mum!' Atlanta insisted, slightly confused, not able to grasp the situation. Then it struck her. How long had she been gone? Trips were only supposed to take a few minutes in normal time, but with all the problems on this trip, she must have been gone for quite some time.

'It's past eight!' Martine snapped, pulling away from the hug. 'You went upstairs five hours ago, and when I go up to see you, you'd disappeared! What was I supposed to think? You didn't say you were going out! I didn't even hear the front door!'

The family and friends behind Martine tutted and cast disapproving looks.

Geneva mouthed, 'you're so dead,' but Atlanta could only glower at her.

'I'm sorry, Mum,' Atlanta said, horrified at the panic she'd obviously caused. She would have to be much more careful when she time travelled again. If she time travelled again. She wasn't sure she would after all this trouble.

'It was so hot,' she fibbed, 'and I just wanted to go out for a walk.'

'In your swimming costume?' her mum countered, disbelievingly. 'Without your keys. Why didn't you phone?'

'I was out of credit,' Atlanta said lamely and then added. 'I didn't realise until I tried to phone you. I just lost track of time,' she muttered, which was closer to the truth than anyone could have imagined. Then she thought of a good idea that might, just might get her off the hook: 'I started a composition and I needed to think about the outdoors and the sound of leaves rustling.'

'Ah, you see, the creative spirit,' said Nana Prest-which, who had never got over the fact that her granddaughter had been accepted by, and now attended, one of the most prestigious music schools in the world.

'Just get inside,' her mum grumbled, more from relief than anger. The neighbours murmured their excuses and left, leaving offers to help if the family needed anything else. Disappointed that there would be no public telling off, Geneva went back to texting on her phone, and followed Lincoln back into the lounge. Nana Prestwich made a tutting sound over and over, something she always did when she had some opinion to share, but wanted to be asked about it first. This time, however, Martine was only concerned with Atlanta. She ushered Atlanta upstairs and into her bedroom, where she sat on the bed and patted the duvet next to her, motioning for Atlanta to join her.

Atlanta sat down and rested her head on her mum's shoulder. 'I really am sorry, Mum,' she said, fighting back tears. It had been a long, strange, scary day and the last thing she wanted right now was to be in trouble at home. Mum kissed her gently on the top of her head.

'I know you are, love,' she said, quietly. 'I know I worry too much. It's hard for me... after your Dad...'

Martine's voice trailed off, unable to say the words, 'got shot in the street'. Atlanta realised then that her going missing, even for a few hours had brought back painful memories for her mum. Atlanta had been so wrapped up in her adventures that she didn't think how hard it must be for her mum just to let her out of the house on her own, constantly afraid that she'd never come back, like her dad. And yet she never made a fuss when Geneva went to the park with her mates, or when Atlanta took the bus to Simon's. That struck Atlanta as incredibly brave.

'I didn't mean to make you worried,' Atlanta snuffled. 'I just didn't think about it.'

'And I don't want you to!' replied her mum, with forced cheeriness. 'I don't want you, or Geneva or Linc, to have to worry that I'm worrying. You should live your life, do what you need to do, and never let fear hold you back. That's why I try not to say anything.'

Martine stood up then and walked to the door. 'Wait here,' she said, 'I've got something for you.'

Atlanta fell back on her bed and looked up at the lampshade hanging from the ceiling. It was covered in cartoon animals, all playing different musical instruments. She'd had it since she was little, when she'd first shown a talent for music. Seeing it now somehow felt even more comforting. She rolled over onto her stomach and buried her face in her duvet, breathing in the clean smell of home.

'Here, this is for you.' Martine tapped Atlanta on the shoulder. Atlanta rolled over and took the gift. It was the photo she'd seen her mum looking at earlier that day. 'I know we haven't really talked about your dad,' Martine said tenderly, ' but that's going to change. I want you to know just how wonderful he was. And I know he'd have wanted you to have this picture.'

Atlanta couldn't hold back her tears any longer. Happiness and relief burst out of her, with a little sting of sadness as well. She threw her arms around her mum and let it all come flooding out. They hugged and talked until the sun went down, and then Atlanta fell into a deep, happy sleep, warm and content in her own bed at last.

Life returned to normal in the days that followed. Atlanta got back into the routine of violin practice and hanging out with Simon but Geneva and Lincoln became increasingly giddy with excitement as the day of their trip to America drew closer. Every day Martine had to explain to them that not everywhere in America was Disneyland.

A few days after her return, Atlanta decided to call Danny Higgins. He picked up quickly when she phoned and listened for ages while she told about the time stream error. He was quite shocked at what had happened to her and kept asking her over and over if she was alright.

'I do feel OK, Danny, but sometimes the memory of being shut in that dreadful shed, in the dark, hour after hour comes back really strongly.'

'I bet it does. I sometimes find myself almost re-living the experiences I've had in the past. But none of mine have been as tough as the things you've been through on this trip. Call me back any time if you need me, if you're feeling bad or anything. Do you remember what came up on the screen when the time stream malfunctioned?'

'Something about the Bosun Field stability falling.' Atlanta paused, 'and then the words 'quantum lock disengaged'. Do they mean anything to you?'

'No, not a thing.'

Mela kept in touch almost every day, not with anything specifically related to time travel missions, but more like a friend. Atlanta got the impression that Mela felt quite guilty about her time slip experience, and she was touched by her concern. They mostly talked about music. Because of her own great musical talent, Mela understood about the way she had suffered from the sounds made by the machines in the mill.

A more formal message from Mela arrived only days before the family trip to America.

Amazing news, Atlanta! We've been going through the data from your trip to the mill that is now known as Quarry Bank Mill and it's fantastic. Well done! I know the time stream errors were scary but they've given us a much deeper look at this period of history than we expected.

The professors here at SHARP were particularly interested in the material you gathered just before I met you at the church. Esther mentioned a war in America. We believe this referred to the American Civil War, when the North and South of the country fought each other. This is really important stuff, and our archives have almost nothing about it. As yet, we have no operatives in America who can travel back to investigate.

The final words caught Atlanta's attention. Her experience with the time stream errors had made her nervous about more voyages back in time, and she'd wondered what she would say if Mela came to her with another mission. She never wanted to feel that scared again, but at the same time the thought of never revisiting the past again was something she found hard to contemplate.

She sent a message back to Mela.

Mela, I'm going to America this week with my family, to a place called Atlanta (it's where my dad was from). Could I travel back in time while I'm there?

Mela's reply came back in a flash.

Atlanta! You are so amazing! That would be perfect, and from what we know, Atlanta (the place!) played an important part in the Civil War. Are you sure you're ready for another trip? I know the last one didn't work out how we planned...

Atlanta knew she wasn't sure, even though the temptation was still there. She messaged back to say that she was not absolutely sure, but she would think about it.

The day of the flight arrived in a hum of activity. Everyone had to get up really early and drag bulging suitcases out to the taxi that would take them to Manchester Airport. Atlanta was a bit worried that her violin would be damaged by being bundled inside an aeroplane with lots of heavy bags, but her mum had insisted she bring it so that her cousins and aunties in America could hear her play. Atlanta just hoped the large, red FRAGILE sticker on the case would be enough to make sure it was packed with care.

The approach to the airport itself was a maze of roundabouts, and as they swung around them on the way to Terminal 1, Atlanta saw a brown sign pointing off in the opposite direction to Quarry Bank Mill. She strained against her seatbelt to see it as the taxi drove past.

'You alright, love?' asked her mum.

'Yeah,' said Atlanta. 'It's just that sign. 'Quarry Bank Mill', I think I've been there.'

'You have, but you wouldn't remember it. You were only just a year old at the time. We took you there, your dad and I for a day out. You cried your eyes out when they showed the old machines working, they made such a noise!'

Atlanta laughed. That explained her strange

sense of having been there before when she'd walked down to the mill with the other apprentices. So those awful machines had always scared her!

At the airport, there was a lot of waiting in lines. First they had to send their luggage rolling along a conveyor belt and through a mysterious rubber curtain. Atlanta held her breath as her violin vanished into the darkness, but the woman at the desk promised her it would be safe. Then they had to queue again to go to the departure lounge, where they had to wait for over an hour to board their flight. Finally, it was time to line up again to get on the plane. It was only when she sat inside the large, metal sausage that Atlanta's excitement began to grow. She was thrilled as the engines roared and the plane thundered down the runway. Lincoln had bagsied the window seat, but Atlanta peered past him and watched in amazement as the airport dropped away beneath them. She felt a weird plunge in her tummy as gravity tried, but failed, to keep them on the ground. Now they were up in the air, it felt like the plane was travelling very slowly, even though Atlanta knew they must be going at hundreds of miles an hour. As it banked around, dipping its wing down so it could circle away from Manchester and off towards America, Atlanta was sure she could see a familiar rectangular building, nestled in a valley, close to the airport.

She thought back to the simple life that Esther and Lucy had led, and wondered what they would have made of this enormous, metal bird that would carry her across the Atlantic Ocean in a matter of hours. But that adventure was over and her next was just beginning.

CHAPTER 12

Atlanta In Atlanta

After the excitement of take-off, the flight to America was boring. Before long, the ground disappeared beneath a blanket of cloud, and all that could be seen from the window was a vast white landscape that looked like it was carved from marshmallow. There was a small screen in the back of each seat and Lincoln soon discovered he could play video games on it. Geneva used hers to watch some movies, while Martine read a book. Atlanta flicked through the films and TV shows she could choose from, but none of them really appealed. Finally, she discovered the plane also had music channels, including one playing classical music, so she plugged in her headphones and zoned out to the sounds of Puccini, Bach and Liszt.

It was a long flight – over eight hours – but Atlanta was lucky that she had the ability to lose herself in music. She dozed without ever really falling asleep, and although she could feel Lincoln fidgeting on one side and Geneva grumbling on the other, nothing could pop her bubble.

Before they knew it, America was rushing up to greet them, an enormous sprawl visible through the gaps in the clouds. The landing was a little more scary than the take-off, as the plane gave a bump and a bounce and its wheels touched the tarmac of the runway. Soon enough, though, it rolled to the terminal and passengers were filing off, stretching and rubbing life back into cramped legs and necks. After even more queuing, to get past an intimidating desk where a stern-faced man checked their passports and to collect their suitcases off a revolving carousel, Atlanta and her family finally emerged into the main airport. They looked for Aunt Bernie. Suddenly Martine started waving and walking towards a tall woman.

Aunt Bernie was a broad, beaming sort of person, her dark brown face sat on top of a bright yellow blouse, while green trousers came to just below her knees. She wasn't fat, she just seemed larger than life, with a big personality that filled the space around her. She had a clutch of bangles on each wrist, and four or five necklaces all made from polished stones or wooden beads. Upon seeing Atlanta's mum, she threw her arms wide and boomed; 'MARTINE, MY DARLING!' at the top of her voice. Atlanta was stunned and little embarrassed. She could tell that her mum felt self-conscious and a bit overwhelmed.

Aunt Bernie ushered them all out to the car park – or parking lot, as she called it – and as soon as they stepped outside, the heat almost knocked Atlanta off her feet. This wasn't the crisp heat of the Manchester summer they'd left behind, with its cool breezes and spots of cloud, it was a thick, clammy heat that made the air feel heavy, like a hot towel wrapped around the face.

'Don't worry, children!' smiled Aunt Bernie. 'We've got air conditioning in the car. We'll soon have it as cold as Manchester, just how you like it!'

Aunt Bernie's car was as big as its owner, a long, wide box on wheels with a back seat broad enough so that all three children could sit on it without rubbing elbows. Atlanta's feet barely reached the floor. As they drove from the airport out to the suburbs, where Aunt Bernie lived, in a place called Sandy Springs, Atlanta watched the highway roll past, quietly marvelling at the fact that all these people, in all these cars, were American. It was such a silly thing to think, but like so many English children, she'd grown up picturing America as a glamorous place that existed on TV and in movies. Seeing it up close, it seemed so normal and yet strangely exotic, the different road signs and billboards made even the most boring scenery thrilling and new.

The journey to Aunt Bernie's house took just over half an hour, and she talked constantly all the way. The poor Tully family was too exhausted, both by the long flight and the sweltering heat, to put up any resistance.

Finally they pulled up at a house in a leafy suburb. Even this, Atlanta realised, was enormous, at least by their standards. Having come from a smallish terraced house in Moss Side, Manchester, Aunt Bernie's house looked like a mansion, with its massive garden, a porch larger than Atlanta's bedroom and a front door the size of a school dining table.

'You must be well rich!' gasped Geneva. Mum hushed her and told her not to be rude, but Aunt Bernie just laughed.

'Not quite, sweetheart! We just build 'em big over here. We've got a lot more space to fill!'

The family was ushered inside, where a dozen more people waited to greet them. By now all four of them were ready to collapse, so Aunt Bernie hurriedly introduced them to a bewildering array of cousins, second cousins, aunts, uncles, great uncles and friends of the family. Raymond, Lissette, Dwight, Carlton, Tyler – the names passed by in a blur of smiles and handshakes, and Atlanta knew she'd never remember half of them.

Eventually, the crowd left with promises of a return visit the following day, and Aunt Bernie showed everyone upstairs to their bedrooms. Atlanta's room was bright and airy, and pleasantly cool. The house had air conditioning – something Atlanta had only ever experienced in supermarkets and cinemas – so it felt like there was an open fridge right behind you wherever you stood. She dropped her suitcase in the corner and carefully laid her violin case, which had survived the flight unscathed, on a desk in the corner. There were framed posters on the wall, old posters for music concerts and album releases, showing men with guitars and trumpets and names like Muddy Waters, John Lee Hooker and Blind Lemon Jefferson. That last one made Atlanta giggle.

'Maybe you'll have your name on a poster like that one day, hmm?' Aunt Bernie was standing at the door watching Atlanta. Her big booming grin had gone and was replaced with a smaller, gentler smile. 'You look so much like him, you know. He'd be proud to know you grew up to play. So very proud.' She looked a little bit sad now. Atlanta realised that while she'd only ever thought of her dad as her father, he'd had a whole life before England that she knew almost nothing about. Aunt Bernie suddenly seemed less like someone she'd been told about, like a character in a story, and became a real person, with a life that over-lapped her own.

'I wish I'd known my dad.' Atlanta hadn't meant to speak, but the words popped out anyway, as if her brain had decided this thought was too important to keep inside.

'You will, darling,' nodded Aunt Bernie. 'This was his room, back when we was growing up. Our daddy built this house with his own hands. Even after Charles moved to England, we kept it the way he liked it. After he died...' She paused here, sighing slightly. 'Well, I just couldn't bring myself to change a thing.'

Atlanta was tired and weary, and it felt weird to hear someone talking about her dad, calling him by his first name. She wanted to hear more, but it was too much right now. Thankfully, Aunt Bernie sensed this.

'I'll leave you to unpack,' she smiled, and headed downstairs. Atlanta slumped onto the bed. She tried to muster the energy to sort out her clothes, but the effort was too much. She slipped into a blissful doze and dreamed of old-fashioned ska music.

CHAPTER 13

The Family Album

Atlanta woke early the next morning. She checked her watch, which her mum had set to local time after landing, and it was five o'clock in the morning, but to her it felt much later. What had been breakfast time in Manchester was now the early hours of the morning.

Realising she wouldn't be able to get back to sleep, she got up and began going through her suitcase, putting her clothes away. Tucked inside an old t-shirt was the time/space travel bag, with her phone. She pressed the power button but when the screen lit up, it simply said 'No signal'. Did that mean Mela wouldn't be able to reach her? Atlanta had no idea how normal mobile phones worked when you were abroad, never mind ones that had been modified with future technology.

It didn't take her long to put her things away, so she took a look around the room. It was amazing to think that her dad had slept under this same roof when he was her age. There was a small bookshelf on the far wall, and since nobody else seemed to be stirring yet, she browsed the spines. There were lots of books about music and musicians, but only a few of which she had heard.

On the bottom shelf, under some old guitar magazines, she spotted a photo album. Flicking through it, she found pictures of a little boy she knew must be her dad and a girl who had Aunt Bernie's unmistakable grin. There were other children as well, seven or eight in all, playing on lawns, riding bicycles and one of them all, standing in a stiff row, smartly dressed, smiling at the camera. She could see that her dad and Aunt Bernie were two of the youngest, and were trying not to laugh. The pictures were faded. Atlanta thought they looked like little windows into the past. She flicked through the pages for hours, so absorbed in the photos that she didn't hear the bedroom door open.

'Oh, you found the family album,' said Aunt Bernie, startling Atlanta.

'Sorry! I wasn't being nosey!' replied Atlanta, suddenly aware that she'd been rummaging in somebody else's things.

'Don't you worry none,' beamed her aunt, 'I was going to show you those pictures today anyway.'

'Who are all those other children?' asked Atlanta,

pointing to the group photo.

'Cousins mostly. The boy on the far end was my other brother, Maurice. He joined the Army.'

'Did he...' Atlanta began forming a question she didn't know how to finish.

'Die? Yes, I'm afraid he did,' said Aunt Bernie. 'No sense in hanging on to sad thoughts, though. It's the happy ones that keep them alive in here.' She tapped a finger to her chest, over her heart. 'That's what makes your daddy's passing so sad. You were so young, you didn't get to store up any happy memories to carry with you.'

Atlanta had never thought of it that way, but despite knowing her for less than a day, Aunt Bernie had put into words the vague feeling that Atlanta had wrestled with for years.

'Come now,' said Aunt Bernie. 'Seems we're the only early birds so what say you help me fix breakfast?'

Atlanta followed Aunt Bernie down to her kitchen. She helped her make pancakes and waffles, pouring special batter mixture into a strange contraption that cooked it into grid patterns. She watched as Aunt Bernie whisked and cooked scrambled eggs with paprika, fried long streaky rashers of bacon and crisped mushrooms on a heavy griddle pan. She served it all up on large white plates while Atlanta went to the fridge – a staggering double-doored beast of an appliance that was larger than Atlanta's wardrobe at home – and took out a huge jug of fresh orange juice.

The delicious smell soon brought the others from upstairs, and they all sat down to this generous breakfast. Lincoln, feeling fussy, turned his nose up at the mountain of cooked food but was overjoyed to discover that American breakfast cereals came in a dizzying variety of sweet flavours and some even came with marshmallow, chocolate and candy pieces. Wide-eyed, he quickly polished off two bowls of brightly coloured Froot Loops.

Aunt Bernie told them she had planned a big barbecue that evening, at which Atlanta was alarmed to learn that she was expected to give a performance on her violin. But there still remained the question of what to do during the day. The news that there was a shopping mall outside of town made Geneva's eyes light up; the idea of going to a proper American mall, like the girls in her favourite TV shows, filled her with excitement. Lincoln, already bursting with energy from his sugary breakfast, almost exploded from his seat when Aunt Bernie described Six Flags Over Georgia, the nearest theme park, which had both Batman and Superman rides.

'What do you like to do, Atlanta?' Aunt Bernie asked. Atlanta really wasn't sure. She was just happy and excited to be in America, and to be meeting her family, and she said so. This made Aunt Bernie smile even more, if that was possible.

Everyone helped to tidy away the breakfast things, and then headed back to their bedrooms to get dressed. The plan was decided. Aunt Bernie had arranged for some of her teenage nieces to take Geneva to the mall, while Mum and Aunt Bernie took Lincoln to Six Flags. Atlanta hadn't decided which one she would do yet. She wasn't really a 'hanging out at the mall' person, but nor did she enjoy roller coasters and theme parks all that much.

As she was getting dressed, Atlanta absent-mindedly checked her phone. To her surprise, there was something on the screen.

‹Signal test. Key operative code to confirm›

She typed in 15799 and hit *send*. When she came back from brushing her teeth, there was another message flashing.

Atlanta, so glad we've been able to make contact. After a lot of experimentation and recalibration, we have another mission lined up. As you know, we can generally only send people back to places they've already visited, which causes a bit of a problem since you've never been to America before.

However, SHARP has been able to deepen the focus of the time stream, and it looks like we'll be able to use key genetic sequences to send you back. Basically, you may not have been to America before but because you have ancestors from there, we've found a window we can use. It won't stay open for long though. If you're going to do this, it has to be in the next few hours.

I know we are asking a lot of you, especially after the problems on the Styal trip, but this would be our first look into American history and could play a huge part in SHARP's mission to rebuild the future. If you are ready and willing, you know what to do!
Mela

Atlanta thought fast. Everyone else was going out, so she could have the house to herself, but wouldn't that look a little rude? Then she had an idea. She quickly threw on some jeans and a t-shirt and met the others in the hallway.

'Are you sure, love?' asked Martine, after Atlanta had explained why she didn't want to go to the mall or the theme park. 'You'll miss all the fun.'

'It's OK, Mum,' Atlanta replied. 'I'm still quite tired and it's been ages since I had a proper practice. And besides, I really need to make sure the violin is in tune if I'm going to play for everyone tonight. If I get bored, I can watch some TV or read a book.'

'Well, if you're sure, and if it's OK with Aunt Bernie,' said Martine, uncertainly.

'It's fine, it's fine,' said Aunt Bernie with a wink. As the others walked outside into the already-sweltering morning sunshine, Aunt Bernie put her hand gently on Atlanta's shoulder. 'I know why you want some time alone,' she said. Atlanta felt a moment of alarm and then Aunt Bernie added, 'You want to spend some more time looking through your daddy's things, right? Well, you make yourself right at home. There's food in the fridge, and if you've got any questions when we come back, I'll be happy to answer them.' And with that, Aunt Bernie bundled everyone else into her enormous car and drove off with a cheerful honk of the horn. As she watched the car drive up the street, Atlanta felt a curious mixture of nerves and excitement. She'd been trusted home alone lots of times in England, but this was America, a whole new country. It made her feel very grown up.

She ran upstairs, changed into her swimming costume, checked that the camera disc was in the time/space travel bag and pushed it tightly to her stomach. Her phone was already buzzing.

Hi, Atlanta,

Here are the details for your mission. It will be a difficult one, I'm afraid. You're travelling back to a time when people were bought and sold because of the colour of their skin. You may find some of the things you experience upsetting. It's important that this time is not forgotten though, so we need you to gather as much information as you can about this time period and what life was like.

Mission details will follow. I'm sure you'll do great.

Mela

‹Time Zone›

November 18th, 1864.

<Place>

Mansfield, Georgia, USA.

<Landing>

Woodland.

<Destination>

Burge Plantation, a cotton plantation owned and run by Dolly Burge.

<Identity>

Mattie, an 11-year-old slave left homeless by the war.

<Conditions>

Extremely dangerous. The country is at war. The Southern states are resisting laws from the government in the North that would make it illegal to own slaves. In an attempt to break the rebel support, the Union forces of the government, led by General Sherman, are moving through the Atlanta area, freeing slaves and destroying property and businesses as they go. The Burge Plantation is in their path.

<Instructions>

Retrieve period clothing from behind the nearest tree.

Follow path to Burge Plantation and ask to be taken in.

‹Equipment›

Mobile phone. Travel bag. Phone fitted with beam of light for emergency use only. Activate by keying in T-O-R-C-H.

If you are ready to travel, do as follows:
›Take off clothing, except for underwear or swimming costume.
›Press the time/space travel bag to your body until it attaches.
›Key in 15799 and press the green button to go.

Good luck.

Atlanta swallowed hard. She'd learned about slavery in history lessons at school, and it had sounded horrible! Did she want to experience it first-hand? At the same time, she knew she had survived the terrible conditions at Styal. Surely she could handle this? Not only that, but Mela was relying on her and, she had to admit, she was deeply curious to see where the cotton she had tried to weave had come from. She also wanted to know how a war could cause mills thousands of miles away to close down. She entered the code but her finger stopped, hovering just over the green button. Acting on an impulse she didn't fully understand, she put the phone down and searched her coat pockets. She pulled out the photo of her dad and placed it carefully in her travel bag.

That done, she pressed the green button and waited for the high-pitched whine to envelope her. It rose and rose and then...Nothing.

CHAPTER 14

Burge Under Siege

Even before Atlanta opened her eyes, the smell of smoke and distant shouts filled her senses. She was in a thick copse of trees. Tall, straight trunks, with branches barren and bony, stretched towards a grey, wintry sky, their roots buried in hard soil of a deep reddish-orange colour. There was nobody in sight, but through the trees, Atlanta caught glimpses of fires burning not far in the distance.

She pushed aside her fear and looked around for the clothing that had been left for her. She quickly spotted the bundle and dressed in a hurry. The clothes were not unlike the ones she had worn at Mr Greg's mill, except harder, scratchier and patched together. That done, she pressed the camera disc to her forehead and slipped the silver backing and her mobile safe into the time/space travel bag under the clothes. She found the path leading from the wood and followed it, nervously looking around at every far off cry. More than once she heard twigs and branches cracking behind her, and whirled around in fright, only to see nothing was there. It wasn't just that this was a stark and fore-boding landscape, it was the sense that something terrible was unfolding around her, the details hidden by walls of skeletal trees and brittle shrubs.

As she hiked through the desolate scrub, she came to a deserted farmyard. It had been wrecked, probably some days earlier. The mud was churned up with dozens of boot prints, and a fire had been left to burn itself out over by an empty pigpen. Something on the ground caught her attention; a child's rag doll. It was a scruffy thing, its threads worn bare from years of play and, no doubt, several days lying outside. Atlanta thought it looked very sad, its black, button eyes looking so lost and forgotten, but she didn't pick it up, after all, who could she return it to?

The path soon grew wider until it looked more like an actual road, and not far along it she came to a small wooden house, raised off the ground on stacks of brick. A chimney was stuck to the right hand side and lazy plumes of smoke wafted into the winter air, while a rough, shingled porch was held up with poles over the front door. Outside, however, there was much activity. People ran back and forth, carrying baskets and sacks, black faces shiny with sweat from the exertion. On the veranda of the house stood a white woman, clearly in charge, with a girl who was maybe a few years younger than Atlanta.

Atlanta approached the woman, dodging through the hectic panic as she went. The woman had an oddly boyish face, handsome rather than pretty. Her clothes were better tailored than those of her slaves, but signs of wear and tear made Atlanta realise that there was a very thin line between rich and poor here. The girl was obviously her daughter, sharing the same serious expression and broad features, though her cheeks were streaked with tears and her shoulders rose and fell with quiet, gasping sobs.

'Excuse me,' Atlanta said, as she came close. The woman, wrapped up in her emergency, hadn't noticed her. She looked down at Atlanta with surprise.

'Who are you, child?' she asked. 'Who do you belong to?'

The question took Atlanta aback. Even though she knew about slavery, it was very strange and unpleasant for someone to ask her who she belonged to. It made her feel for a moment as if she really was just a 'belonging'.

'My name is Mattie and I have nowhere to go,' Atlanta replied, having rehearsed the story in her mind. 'My home has been burned down and I've been wandering in the woods. I was hoping I could stay here.'

The woman's face softened immediately. 'Then you may call me Miss Dolly. There's room for you here, Mattie, but you must help us prepare. The blue coats are coming back and we must hide as much of the food and clothing as we can, before they take it all.'

Atlanta nodded. Dolly handed her a heavy sack. 'Take this oatmeal,' Dolly insisted. 'Take it through the yard and out to the back. The boys there are hiding our supplies until the soldiers have passed.' She waved a young boy over and gave him another sack. ' Jack, take this to your father in the yards. This is Mattie, she'll be helping you.'

'Yes, ma'am,' nodded Jack politely, and motioned for Atlanta to follow him as he hoisted the sack onto his shoulders with thin, wiry arms. Atlanta could barely lift hers off the ground, so she waddled off in pursuit, the heavy sack dragging and scuffing along the floor. She followed Jack around the house and passed through a yard where turkeys and pigs were shuffling nervously in their pens. Sure enough, she found a group of men, hard at work trying to hide all manner of food. Some was being buried in boxes, some was hidden in the animal feed, more still was arranged under a large sheet, with leaves and branches arranged on top to disguise it from prying eyes. Atlanta saw cuts of meat wrapped in cloth, barrels of salt and what looked like churns of butter.

One group of men struggled with large bundles of white fluff that looked very familiar. She went closer to investigate. The material was soft to the touch, and when she pinched a little between her fingers she realised it was cotton, raw cotton just like she had seen at the mill. This cotton, she realised, would be shipped over to England, where the mills of Lancashire would first spin it into threads, then weave it into cloth. Picked by slaves in one country and woven by apprentices in another, Atlanta thought. Only now, because of the war, the cotton was not getting picked or shipped, which meant the mills were closing down. Everything was connected, she understood.

She looked around at the commotion and decided that, apart from the colour of their skin, the slaves on the plantation had a lot in common with the workers in the mill. They all worked incredibly hard for someone else, relying on them for food and shelter, and they would all be punished for any failing in their duties. The big difference, she thought, was that at least back in England apprentices like Lucy and Esther were free once their contract with Mr Greg was completed. These slaves belonged to their owners forever, no different to the pigs and turkeys. A hot surge of anger flushed her cheeks at the injustice of it.

'Watch yourself, child!'

She moved out of the way as a thick-set man, his dark skin etched with lines, his close-cropped hair greying at the temples, walked past leading a horse. The man's forehead was beaded with sweat and his hands as dirty as the cuffs of his trousers. The horse could apparently sense the tension in the air; it whinnied and pulled at its reins. The man was trying to calm it down when Miss Dolly joined them. Her daughter, still crying, followed behind.

'How goes the field, Elbert?' she asked the man.

'The men are finished with the plough, Miss Dolly,' he said, his voice a gravely, bass rumble. 'We'll be ready for seeding, so long as Sherman's army doesn't trample it flat again. Mr Ward and Frank are back from hiding the mules.'

'The supplies are all in, Pa,' said Jack. Atlanta realised that they must be father and son. Elbert nodded his approval and patted Jack on the shoulder.

'And do you have any news of the army, Miss Dolly?' Elbert asked.

'Last I heard the Yankees were at Stockbridge, headed for Savannah,' she replied. Atlanta had no idea where these places were, or if this was good news or bad. 'They're gettin' close though. Nute says he was met by two Yankees on the road just yesterday. They told him to join them and was askin' about our livestock. I fear they'll be turnin' their attention our ways soon enough.'

'Least we's prepared,' said Elbert, his face grim.

'Indeed, Elbert, indeed.' Miss Dolly and Elbert fell silent for a moment, as if preparing themselves for a blow they knew would land soon. It was Dolly who broke the silence. 'Sadai and I are headed up to the Perry place to see if they've heard any different,' she said. 'You keep your eye on things here, and make sure the children are safe.'

With that, Dolly and her daughter, headed on through the yard and out towards the road. Elbert turned to Atlanta and Jack.

'Don't recall seeing you round here before,' he said to Atlanta.

'Her farm was looted, Pa,' Jack said, before Atlanta could even answer. 'Name's Mattie. Miss Dolly has said she can stay here till the Yankees pass.'

'Well then I'm mighty pleased to meet you, Mattie,' rumbled Elbert, doing a mock bow that made Atlanta giggle, despite the grim situation. 'Jack, go round up the other children, send 'em home to their cabins before nightfall. Mattie, you're welcome to help him, if you like.'

Elbert strode off in the other direction, no doubt taking the horse somewhere safe, while Jack led Atlanta back towards the Burge house.

'What do the Yankees want?' Atlanta asked Jack as they walked. 'I don't understand what's happening.'

'Pa says they're comin' to free the slaves,' Jack said. 'Not sure what I think of that.' 'Wouldn't that be a good thing?' Atlanta replied. 'Nobody wants to be a slave.'

'Sure,' nodded Jack. 'Bein' made a free man would surely be a fine thing, but I don't reckon either the Yankees or the Rebels are much concerned with what happens to us. Ain't neither of them seems to mind what happens to the poor folk in the middle. We're the ones that gets burned from our homes or dragged away to join some army. Or worse...'

Atlanta shuddered. Her short time at the mill had made her realise how horrible it felt to have no power over your life, and she could barely begin to understand how that must feel for boys like Jack, passed around and used like tools or a piece of furniture, but at the same time she couldn't understand why this General Sherman was leading an army to destroy farms and terrorise ordinary people, rather than fighting against another army on a battlefield.

She and Jack walked around the plantation, finding the children. There was a surprising amount of them, and Atlanta could see they didn't seem to be worked as hard as the apprentices back in the mill. Most had been given jobs tidying or cleaning, the younger ones simply played outside. When they went out in the fields, however, Atlanta could see some of the men returning from working the soil, soaked with sweat, feet and hands swollen with blisters. Once Jack was old enough, she reckoned, he'd be out there as well.

They were just returning to the house when gunshots rang out, big, flat, ugly sounds that punched the air. The younger children began screaming and ran for the house. Miss Dolly and Sadai came running in from the road, breathless. They reached Atlanta and Jack without slowing down, and Miss Dolly urged them into the house as well. Elbert followed close behind.

'What's happenin', Miss Dolly?' he asked, the firmness of his voice sounding slightly forced, as if he were trying very hard not to let his fear show itself.

'Yankees comin' down the hill,' gasped Miss Dolly. 'We were talkin' with Laura Perry up the road, they hit her farm yesterday. Her husband Jim was out with the Home Guard, lookin' for the ones that did it. Then we saw them, marching towards us. The men started shootin' so we got back here as if the devil himself were at our heels.'

There were dozens of people crammed into the house now, talking in whispers and some even praying. Rumours bounced from person to person that some of the slaves had already run off to join Sherman's army before they came and took them. Elbert tried to calm the room down, but panic was already setting in. Atlanta still didn't understand why this was happening. Sherman's army was freeing the slaves, which was good, but they seemed to be doing it in a way that left the people they were saving even more terrified than usual. Miss Dolly owned slaves, which was bad, yet she seemed like a nice, kind lady. None of this made sense. She approached Miss Dolly, who was peering outside to see what was happening.

'Why are they doing this?' Atlanta asked.

'Because they've been told to,' Miss Dolly explained bitterly, hugging Sadai close as she hunched down on the floor below the window. 'The President says we can't own, or buy or sell slaves no more, but some of the states down here in the South don't want to go along with that.'

'But slavery is wrong,' Atlanta blurted out, without thinking. 'Everybody knows that.' This brought sharp gasps and mutters from the others in the room, some murmuring cautious agreement, others shocked that she had dared to say such a thing to Miss Dolly.

'You certainly are forthright with your views, Mattie,' Miss Dolly said, quite calmly. 'Reckon your master had more than a few troubles with you. But I don't entirely disagree. Slaves is simply how it is down here. How we always done things. Most folks don't know any different and change scares them. For my part, I haven't bought or sold a slave since my husband passed, when I inherited this plantation. If the law says the slaves should be free, I don't reckon I'll argue against that.'

'So couldn't you just set them free now?' Atlanta said. 'Wouldn't the soldiers leave us alone then?'

'I don't reckon so,' Miss Dolly replied with a sad, resigned shrug. 'War's war. There's no taming that beast once it's set loose. This is about more than slaves. Cotton drives the economy of the state. Without trade, the war is over. Don't really matter if good folks or bad get trampled, burned or shot along the way, I guess.'

Atlanta didn't want to be trampled, or burned, and especially not shot. She instinctively felt through her clothes for her phone, ready to key in her code and be whisked back home. Instead, her fingers found the photo of her dad, tracing the stiff edges of the picture through her dress. For some reason, that made her feel braver.

Just then, one of the slaves burst in through the door in a panic. 'They're at the gate!' he cried. 'They're comin' in!'

CHAPTER 15

Eli And The Doll

Atlanta peered over the windowsill and saw dozens of soldiers pouring through the gate to the plantation and running up the path towards the house. Each one carried a rifle with a fierce looking blade attached to the barrel, and some even had swords hanging from their belts. Atlanta ducked down again quickly.

It was as if electricity had bolted through the room. Everyone jumped and scrambled backwards away from the door. Dolly and Elbert tried their best to keep them calm, but soon the soldiers had reached the house and could be seen by everybody as they rampaged through the plantation. Further down, on the road, hundreds more men in General Sherman's army could be seen marching past, a procession of dark blue and steel that seemed to never end. The door to the house was forcefully pushed open and in came a man, tall and severe in his uniform, his face bristling with a neatly clipped moustache and beard. Miss Dolly rose to greet him, holding her head up high defiantly. The man snapped to attention before her.

'Ma'am,' he said. 'I am Captain Webber of the Union Army.'

Dolly glared at him. 'I am Dolly Lunt Burge, sole owner and proprietor of this plantation and I claim protection from these vandals,' she almost spat this word, 'who are even now forcing themselves into my rooms.'

Captain Webber relaxed his posture and nodded thoughtfully.

'Burge, you say. I believe I knew your brother, Orrington, over in Chicago, Miss Burge. It surely is a shame that so many friends and brothers find themselves enemies because of this war. I can promise you that your house will be untouched, but I cannot vouch for your outbuildings, nor any slaves still residing there. Those able-bodied young men who do not choose to join our march may be taken by force.'

This last remark caused some of the slaves in the house, parents of those still at the cabins, to cry out in horror. Dolly's shoulders slumped. 'Then that will have to be sufficient,' she said. 'You, at least, have behaved like a gentleman.' Captain Webber clicked his heels, nodded curtly and left. A mixture of relief and frantic worry filled the room. They were safe in here, but what would be left of the plantation by the time the soldiers left was another matter. An uneasy silence fell, broken only by the noise of buildings being torn down outside, and the horrible sound of gunshots and animal screams as the soldiers killed Dolly's livestock for food.

'Where's Sadai?' It was Dolly who shattered the silence with her panicked cry. Her daughter had been sitting in the corner before, but was nowhere to be seen now. One of the slaves, a teenage girl called Lydia, meekly raised her hand and confessed that she had seen Sadai sneaking out of the room while Dolly was talking to the captain. A search of the house followed, but there was still no sign of the girl.

'I declare, she's gone looking for that blasted doll,' Dolly fretted. 'She's not stopped pecking at me about it all day. Convinced some soldier took it and threw it in woods yonder.' This caught Atlanta's attention. Could the doll she had seen on the ground at the other place be the doll Sadai was looking for?

Elbert got to his feet. 'I'll go and look for her, Miss Dolly,' he said.

'No, Elbert,' Dolly replied, reluctantly. 'I need you here, and I couldn't bear it if those soldiers took you with them.'

'I'll go,' Atlanta said, much to the surprise of everyone in the room, most of whom didn't even know who this strange girl was. 'I can move quickly and stay out of sight, and I think I know where she'll be looking.' Miss Dolly looked at Atlanta, then out of the window at the soldiers. She clearly didn't like the idea, but she nodded her approval. Atlanta made her way to the back door of the house and peered out. She could see soldiers over in the yard, tearing apart the hiding places and dragging the supplies away, but if she moved fast she could make it to the back wall and cut across to the road without being seen.

She waited for an opening, eased the door open and raced for the wall, crouching low. The next part was trickier, because she had to crawl past the fence, only a few feet away from a group of soldiers who were arguing about tobacco rations. Slowly and carefully, she dragged herself along the dusty ground. Evening was drawing in, which gave Atlanta more shadows to hide in, but also made her more scared. Searching for Sadai in the dark would not be easy. Inch by inch, she pulled herself along. Suddenly, footsteps were approaching, crunching on the brittle grass. Atlanta froze in place at the base of the fence, pressing her face into the dust. She could see the soldier's boots, less than twelve inches from where she lay, hidden only by the thin branches of a dying shrub. The stink of smoke wafted down to her as the soldier lit a pipe. The fence creaked as he leaned on it, unaware of the child on the other side. She held her breath, her body trembling with fear. Her heartbeat pounded in her head like a drum.

Finally, somebody shouted and the soldier moved away, back towards the house. Atlanta waited for a minute or so, then carefully got to her knees and looked around. There was now a hundred feet or so between her and the nearest soldiers, so she took a deep breath and made a dash for the road. She felt certain that her feet pounding the dry ground must sound like thunderclaps, and with every step she expected a large hand to fall on her shoulder. Somehow, it didn't happen and she made it to the edge of the plantation without being caught.

At the road, Atlanta found that the stream of soldiers had slowed down. The large platoon that had just marched past was now walking away from her, while the next group was only just coming into view up the hill. She quickly darted across the road and began making her way towards the path that led into the woods. Doubts began to build in the back of her mind. What if Sadai hadn't come out here after all? But she pressed on into the woods until she heard a noise from up ahead. Atlanta stopped dead in her tracks and listened. Whoever it was, they were crying, a young girl's cry. It had to be Sadai. Atlanta headed for the sound, and sure enough, there was the missing girl. She was looking from left to right, searching in the fading light for her lost doll.

'Hey,' Atlanta whispered, but even that made Sadai jump. 'It's OK,' Atlanta continued. 'I've come to take you home.'

'But my doll... I need my doll. I know I dropped it in the woods somewhere,' Sadai moaned. Atlanta took her by the hand. 'Follow me,' she said, and dragged the girl back to the path. From there, Atlanta quickly got her bearings and retraced her steps to the ruined farm where she'd seen the doll earlier that day. Even in the dim light of dusk, she could see it was still there, right where she'd seen it before. She clambered over the splintered fence and picked the doll up, passing it back to Sadai's outstretched hand.

The girl clutched it close to her chest and a huge smile spread over her face.

'Thank you, thank you, thank you, you found my Liza,' she gushed. Sadai was about the same age as

Geneva, Atlanta realised, but she seemed much younger. No television, and no school friends to make her act like a teenager too early.

'Come on,' Atlanta said. 'Let's get you home.'

It was still just light enough to find their way back to the road, and whenever Atlanta felt like she was losing her way in the gloom, she looked up to make sure the moon was still in the same place. It didn't take them long to get back to the road, where they found, to their relief, that the soldiers must have passed. Feeling confident, they walked down the road in the open, not bothering to skulk in the verges. Sadai cooed and murmured to her doll the whole time.

'Now where are you two headed?'

The girls almost jumped out of their skin at the booming voice from behind them. Sadai fumbled and dropped her doll, frantically picking it up again before turning around.

Before them, caught in the moonlight, stood a tall black man, broad shouldered and wearing the distinctive blue Yankee uniform. His arms were folded across his chest, and he looked down at them with one eyebrow raised. Sadai whimpered. Atlanta instinctively stepped forwards, putting herself between the man and the younger girl.

'None of your business,' she snapped. The man laughed, a rich chuckle riding on the cool night air.

'Well now, can't say I can argue with that,' he laughed. 'Ain't none of my business. You got that right.'

'Well then, we'll be on our way,' replied Atlanta. She hoped she sounded confident and grown up, because inside she was absolutely terrified. If the man sensed her act, he didn't let on.

'Now, now,' he said, holding up his hands in mock surrender. 'I don't mean you no harm. I just see two young girls walkin' a road like this in the dark, and I get to worryin'. There's unsavoury folk abroad tonight.'

'We know,' retorted Atlanta. 'They attacked our home, and you're wearing the same uniform.'

'Hmm,' the man said, nodding slowly. 'I won't make excuses or apologise for the lack of courtesy that General Sherman's men have shown you. Truth is, they've not been much kinder to me. But they do fight for a cause more important than the actions of any one man, and maybe when you're old enough to have children of your own, you'll understand why.'

'Then explain it to me,' Atlanta demanded. 'Please,' she added, rather sheepishly. She couldn't keep up this tough act and there was something about the man that made her feel comfortable.

'What do you say I walk you home?' said the man. 'You can call me Eli, if you please.'

'Atlanta,' said Atlanta. She bit her tongue. She'd given her real name! If Sadai picked up on the mistake, she didn't seem to react. The man, however, found it very amusing.

'Atlanta, huh?' he laughed, another chuckle rolling up from his belly and out into the night. 'Well that's a mighty fine name, indeed. Guess I don't need to ask where you from then.'

The curious trio began walking again, with Eli a few steps behind the girls. Soon the gate of the Burge Plantation was in sight. There were no fires, at least, but broken wood and shattered stone spilled out into the road from where the soldiers had torn their way through the buildings. And there, at the gate, Miss Dolly, Elbert and some of the others were waiting for them. Sadai ran to them, her doll dangling by its leg in her hand.

'I don't understand,' Atlanta said, as they watched Sadai reunited with her mother. 'Why destroy these farms? Why are you scaring people like Miss Dolly? She's a nice person.'

'Miss Dolly owns the plantation, yes? Those are her slaves?' Eli asked in reply.

'Well, yes,' said Atlanta. She wished she could untangle the confusion she felt. 'But she's not mean, and she wants to look after them.'

'Well, that's mighty decent,' said Eli, rubbing his fingers across his chin. It was quiet enough on the road that Atlanta could her the scratch and scrape of his whiskery beard. 'And I don't doubt this Miss Dolly is a fine, upstanding Christian woman who means nobody no harm. It's good that she looks after her people, but there's plenty more that don't. Believe me.'

He stopped, turned away from Atlanta and lifted his shirt. His back was criss-crossed with thick, ugly scars, the hard puckered flesh like tiny mountain ranges rising from his skin. Atlanta gasped in horror.

'Fifty lashes,' Eli explained. 'Master took it upon himself to teach me a lesson for lookin' him in the eye when he wasn't in the right mood. And I got off light. I seen folk whipped within an inch of their life, beaten with iron bars. Things so bad it ain't right to talk about them in front of a young girl.'

He pulled his shirt down and clumsily tucked it into his belt with shaking fingers. The smile had gone from his face, replaced with a hollow, haunted expression that chilled Atlanta to the bone. Eli crouched down with his hands on his knees.

'Listen now, I don't much care for the politics and fancy talk,' he said, his voice quiet and thoughtful. 'I don't agree with all this burnin' and lootin', but it ain't my place to say otherwise. Fact is, sometimes people do bad things because they chasin' a good cause. Don't excuse it, but that's how it is. And sometimes good people do bad things 'cause they don't know no better. It's just how they been raised, how the world is, and nobody seen fit to stand up and say it's wrong. And folk like you and me,' he fixed Atlanta with a meaningful stare, 'we get caught in the middle, and that's a hell of a place to be. Gets so you can't tell which way is up and which is down. All you can do is keep your eye on the thing you want most. The thing you're fightin' for.'

'What's that?' asked Atlanta, her throat dry.

'Freedom,' Eli said. His gaze shifted, his eyes grew wet and it seemed to Atlanta that he was looking at something far away, over her shoulder.

'I don't want to be whipped or beaten,' Eli said, almost to himself, 'but I don't want to be owned, or looked after neither. Not by anybody, no matter their skin. I want to plough my own land, grow my own crops and raise a family. And I want my children to do the same, and their children and on and on until the good Lord comes a-callin' for us all.' Eli shook his head, as if rousing himself from a daydream, and stood up, clearing his throat with a gruff cough.

'That's all I want,' he said.

Atlanta could only nod. She felt like her head had been stuffed with ideas, some of them too big to consume right now, but something, deep inside, had clicked. Not just for the people on Burge plantation but for the people at Quarry Bank Mill as well. It made her own life – her cosy, comfortable modern life – seem very lucky and special.

She felt grateful, and also more responsible. Grown up, even. She promised herself, there and then, never to take anything for granted again. Not just things like TV and mobile phones, but the simple fact that she could sleep in on Saturdays, that she could go to school and play the violin, that she had decades ahead of her to decide who and what she wanted to be. She had to make the most of that opportunity, not for herself but for people like Eli and Jack, Lucy and Esther, and the millions of other people over the centuries whose lives were written in stone because of where and when they lived. If she wasted these chances, she would be letting them all down. As if on cue, she felt the familiar buzz of her mobile phone against her stomach. It was time to go home.

She didn't know how to begin explaining that to Eli, so she simply said, 'thank you,' instead. Eli smiled and nodded in the direction of the plantation gates.

'You better hurry along now as well,' he said. 'It's gettin' late.'

'Oh, I'm not going back there,' replied Atlanta. 'I live somewhere else. Don't worry, I can get there by myself. It's not very far away. Well, actually, it's very far away, but not how you think. It's hard to explain.'

Eli looked at her, confused. The corners of his mouth crinkled into a smile. 'You sure are a strange one, Miss Atlanta,' he told her, placing one of his big, rough hands on her cheek. 'I get the feelin' you gonna be someone real special when you grow up. You take care now, you hear?'

Atlanta blushed. She watched as Eli walked off down the road, giving a friendly nod and wave to Miss Dolly and the others as he passed. While they were distracted, and before Miss Dolly or Sadai could see her, Atlanta ducked across the road and into the darkness of the trees on the other side.

She pulled out her phone, but as she did the

photo of her dad came out as well, and fell to the ground. Squinting against the gloom, she fumbled around with her fingers until she found it. Her heart was hammering at the thought of losing it. Now, more than ever, it seemed very important. She carefully placed the photo back into her bag and then removed her borrowed clothes, folding them neatly and leaving them behind a tree. Then she activated her phone. The screen folded open, casting a cold blue glow over her. She keyed in 15799 and pressed the red button.

She heard a far-off whining noise coming closer and closer. Then...nothing.

CHAPTER 16

The Line Of History

Atlanta found herself back in the bedroom at Aunt Bernie's house. She fell back onto the bed and felt the cool cotton against the back of her legs and neck. Cotton. She smiled to herself. She'd never take that material for granted ever again, that was for sure.

She checked the clock on the wall. She'd been gone less than half an hour. Her family wouldn't be back for hours, so she allowed herself the small luxury of lying there a little while longer, letting her thoughts and feelings swirl and settle. There was a hint of sadness, familiar now after four trips back in time, at the thought that the people she'd met in the past had grown old and died in the blink of an eye it took her to return home. Yet there was a sense of fulfilment as well, a feeling of satisfaction that she'd not just seen the past, but touched it, felt it, spoken to it and come back a little wiser.

Eventually, she forced herself upright and removed her travel bag. She took out her phone, and carefully removed the photo of her dad. Knowing that it had travelled with her made her feel happy, for some reason, as if she'd shared the trip with him. Silly, she told herself, but the contented feeling didn't go away. Then she padded across the landing to Aunt Bernie's brilliant white bathroom and showered, letting the tingling hot water wash the 150 year old dust out of her hair and down the plughole.

Dried and dressed, Atlanta quickly tuned her violin – it didn't really need it, but she felt she should after using it as her excuse to stay home – and ran through a few practice scales. Later that afternoon she'd be playing for a garden full of family and friends, but she no longer felt nervous. In fact, she was looking forward to it.

That done, she turned her attention to something that had been gnawing at the back of her mind. She picked up the old family photo album and carried it downstairs. She poured herself a generous glass of orange juice, made herself a chunky sandwich from Aunt Bernie's enormous fridge, and retreated to the lounge. Curled up on the sofa with the only sound a faint hum from the air conditioning to distract her, she opened the album and went through each page methodically, making mental notes of questions she wanted to ask Aunt Bernie.

The list soon grew quite long. The photos of Aunt Bernie and her dad gave way to photos of people she could only guess at. A group of smiling black men, posing in crisp uniforms in front of an old fashioned fighter plane. That would be World War Two, she knew, but who were the men and which one was she related to? Even further back, she found photos of 1920s nightclubs, of a pretty lady in a shop selling shoes and someone leaning on a park bench, cigar jutting proudly from his mouth. And there, right at the back, in a photograph that was almost yellow with age and covered in cracks, she saw something that made her stop in her tracks. She looked again, unable to believe her eyes.

After that discovery, the wait for Aunt Bernie and the others to come home was torture. She tried practicing her violin, but she couldn't focus. She tried watching TV but the channels only showed news and cop shows, and there were adverts every few minutes. She quickly got frustrated and switched it off again. In the end, she simply passed the time by staring at the photo. That maddening, amazing photo.

When she finally heard the key in the door, she jumped up to greet them. Aunt Bernie bustled in first, followed by a weary looking Martine. Lincoln was next, clutching a Superman-shaped helium balloon that bumped and bounced through the door behind him. As they were coming in, Aunt Bernie's teenage nieces pulled up in a rather battered old car and Geneva scrambled out, swishing up the driveway with a swagger she'd obviously learned from copying girls at the mall. She was carrying a shopping bag, so Atlanta figured she'd already used up her holiday spends. It seemed to take an age for everyone to come in and get settled. Martine kicked off her shoes and collapsed on the sofa, while Lincoln excitedly told anyone who'd listen how he'd made her go on his favourite ride four times. Martine looked pleadingly at Atlanta and mimed being sick. Atlanta giggled and shot her a sympathetic look.

'I'll make us some coffee,' Aunt Bernie announced and headed for the kitchen. Atlanta saw her opening. 'I'll help!' she said, a little too quickly, and scooped up the photo album as she followed her aunt. Aunt Bernie had a fancy coffee machine rather than a kettle, and while it made weird bloops and gloops, Atlanta put the album on the worktop.

'You like the album?' Aunt Bernie asked, offering a packet of cookies to Atlanta. She took one gratefully but didn't eat it. She had more important things on her mind.

'I wanted to ask you about some of these people,' Atlanta said. 'Especially...' She flipped through to the back and pointed to the old cracked photo. 'This one.'

The photo showed a tall black man, his shirt sleeves rolled up. He was standing in a field, leaning on a plough, a grumpy looking mule behind him. He was staring into the camera with an easy smile, his brow glistening with sweat. It was a wonderful photo, natural and spontaneous, the look of pride on his face impossible to miss. It was a photo of Eli.

'Well now,' laughed Aunt Bernie. 'You've gone all the way back to the beginning there. Let me see...' Aunt Bernie paused as she worked things out in her head. 'He was my daddy's grandaddy, so he'd be your great, great grandfather, Eli Tully.'

'He was a slave,' said Atlanta, a matter of fact statement, with no question in her voice.

'That's right,' nodded Aunt Bernie. 'Though he wasn't when this photo was taken. This was around 1880, and that's his farm, the start of the Tully family really. He built it all himself, saved the money, worked the land. He...oh, child! What's the matter?'

Atlanta couldn't help herself. Tears were pouring down her face.

'It's just...' she began, but had to choke back the words. 'I'm just happy for him,' she said. 'He got what he wanted.'

Aunt Bernie grabbed Atlanta and hugged her. 'He surely did,' she said softly, 'and you're here to prove it.' Atlanta smiled and wiped her eyes. She looked again at the photo of Eli and felt something inside her change: a hole being filled.

Just then the doorbell chimed and Geneva came bundling into the kitchen.

'They're here!' she shrieked, excitedly. 'Everyone's here!'

Within an hour the house was full of life. Dozens of people came by to meet the Tullys from England, but now, rather than being overwhelmed, Atlanta loved every second of it. A barbecue was lit in the back yard, and soon the delicious smell of ribs and burgers filled the air, to a background buzz of conversation and laughter.

When the sun started to set, Martine took Atlanta aside. 'Are you going to play?' she asked. 'I know Aunt Bernie sort of volunteered you without asking, so I won't mind if you don't feel up to it.'

'No, I want to,' Atlanta replied, slipping an arm around her mum's waist and giving her peck on the cheek. 'I've been looking forward to it.' She raced upstairs, taking the steps two at a time, and took her violin out of its case. She looked down from the bedroom window at the yard below, full of friendly faces, old and young, black and white, all laughing and joking together. This is my family, she thought to herself. A unique, sprawling spider-web of history, traced across centuries and all leading to these people, and this night. It felt good. It felt right. Atlanta smiled the biggest smile her face could handle.

She picked up her violin, went downstairs and began to play.

Collect the other exciting books in the Time Traveller Kids series and discover the history of famous sites in the United Kingdom

Danny's interest in history is zero, but when a mysterious boy, claiming to be from a future organisation called SHARP gets in contact with him on his mobile, Danny agrees to travel back to the Tudor period. Making friends in the long-forgotten past gets him seriously hooked on time travel, not to mention history!

Danny has become an experienced time traveller but this doesn't help him when SHARP's communication systems fail. It is the year 671, the Dark Ages and he is left stranded in the depths of winter when wolves roamed the English countryside and Danny cannot understand a word the strange people speak.

Incredibly musically gifted, Atlanta is entranced by the music of the far-into-the- future humankind. Is this what makes her agree to join the growing band of twenty first century kids who go back in time to gather information for the organisation called SHARP?

When Alex McLean is catapulted back to 1314 by a rival outfit to SHARP, his life is in serious danger. This organisation, called STRAP, do not care if he falls to his death when he joins the desperate band of Scots fighters who did the impossible and scaled the terrifying Rock on which Edinburgh Castle stands to this day.

Jo Kelly's parents, both Oxford Academics, are so busy fussing over her super bright brother, who is a chorister in the world famous Magdalen College choir, that they don't realize they are ignoring Jo. How envious they would be, if they knew that Jo is sent back in time to Oxford 1939 and that she actually meets the legendary C.S. Lewis and J.R. Tolkien.

When ten-year-old Sarah accepts the challenge to travel back in time, she thought that she might meet Robin Hood. She had not bargained on joining a band of half-starved children toiling deep under ground in a south Yorkshire coalmine. She becomes a 'trapper' – a child who pulled a string to open a trap to let the trucks of coal hurtle onwards down the tunnel, that is until the mine started flooding. Sarah's life is in danger!

The Blog

If you've enjoyed this book, go to Danny's Blog for an exciting FREE read.

www.travellingthroughtimeispossible.wordpress.com/

Competitions And Activities

Seven Arches Publishing often runs competitions for you to enter with prizes of book tokens, that can be spent in any bookshop, for solving puzzles or for a good illustration. Why not go to www.sevenarches-publishing.co.uk and check out whether there is competition or activity on its way based on one or other of our books. We often include the winning entries of our competitions, or the writing, poems or pictures that you send us in the next print run of the title.

Contact Us

You are welcome to contact Seven Arches Publishing by:

Phone: 0161 4257642

Or

Email: admin@sevenarchespublishing.co.uk